DATURA

(OR A DELUSION WE ALL SEE)

Datura

or

A Delusion We All See

by Leena Krohn

Translated by

Anna Volmari and J. Robert Tupasela

Cheeky Frawg Books
Tallahassee, Florida

Originally published in 2001 in Finnish as *Datura tai harha jonka jokainen näkee.*

Translation copyright (©) 2013, J. Robert Tupasela and Anna Volmari.

ISBN 978-09857904-6-2

Cheeky Frawg is run by Ann & Jeff VanderMeer.
Editorial Assistance: Desirina Boskovich and John Klima

Cheeky Frawg logo copyright © 2011 by Jeremy Zerfoss
Cover and interior design by Jeremy Zerfoss

Cheeky Frawg would like to thank FILI, the Finnish Language Exchange (http://www.finlit.fi/fili/en/), for partially subsidizing the translation of this book.

For a complete catalogue of Cheeky Frawg selections, visit:
http://www.cheekyfrawg.com

Cheeky Frawg
POB 4248
Tallahassee, FL 32315
pressinfo@vandermeercreative.com

Contents

The Third Seed Pod

THE FIRST SEED POD

A Delusion We All See

I can only blame myself and a certain flower for my current state. Or two flowers, actually.

The first I saw when I was seven years old. Someone had picked some flowers in the garden at our summer house and put them in a vase. The tallest had just opened—incandescent orange with dark leopard spots. The midday sun filled the room and the flower embodied summer lushness. I looked at it and asked my sister what flower it was.

"A crown imperial," she replied.

I couldn't take my eyes off it. I was sure she was right about the name, but I looked at this flower differently than I had at any flower before. A new idea was germinating in my mind, and it made me say, "It might not be a crown imperial."

"It's a crown imperial," she said.

"But it *might* not be," I insisted.

What made me say that? A sudden thought that the flower was unknowable, not just by me, but by anybody, even people who knew its name. But I wasn't able to express this epiphany in a way that other people could understand. I didn't mean that the flower had some other name. What I wanted to say had to do with being, not naming. The name of the flower was something completely arbitrary and beside the point. The flower was not what it was called. Not this flower. Not any flower.

We were misled even by our own perceptions. They revealed hardly anything to us about the true nature of the flower. The essence of the flower—what or who the flower truly was—was somewhere else, is always somewhere else.

"Go ask grandma," my sister said.

I asked. I was sure that grandma would understand what I thought

I now understood.

But grandma also said, "It most certainly is a crown imperial."

Why am I telling you this? Because I then understood that this one flower could not be known, and later I have learned that this same otherness applies to all living things—people, the world, our entire reality. What we are able to perceive—see, hear, smell, and measure—gives us enough information to get by on a daily basis, but too little to understand what everything really means.

Perhaps it was that bit of information that wounded me. Perhaps that was what later made me so vulnerable to seduction by that other flower.

My sister thinks that my bad health is partly due to the people I met while editing *The New Anomalist*. I was infected by their distorted perceptions, that's what she says. The accusation isn't fair. She doesn't know about my relationship to datura. The same flower, tragically enough, that she once gave me with the best of intentions. The damage it caused is permanent.

When I think about datura, I remember the Marquis, the chief editor of *The New Anomalist*, and all the magazine's readers and contributors. I had never known that people could have such odd ideas. Together, the datura and these people formed a new pattern, a wavering structure into which I innocently stepped. It was a trap from which escape would not be easy. In a way I am still fighting for my freedom.

It has been so long now. You'll have to tell me the year, I can't remember today. The flower changed me, my perception of the world, and my sense of time, as well. The world is no longer the same place, and neither am I.

This is what I think I've learned: reality is nothing more than a working hypothesis. It is an agreement that we don't realize we've made. It's a delusion we all see. Yet it's a shared, necessary illusion, the end product of our intelligence, imagination, and senses, the basis of our health and ability to function, our truth.

Hold on to it. It's all—or nearly all—that you have. Try to step outside of it and your life will change irreversibly, assuming you survive at all.

If you want, I'll let you read the notes I made at the time. I've expanded them here to pass the time. They aren't pure diary entries. The dates are missing, and I doubt they're in chronological order. How well these entries describe what really happened isn't any clearer to the writer than they are to the reader. To describe events is to distort them. Like pressing flowers, books preserve the appearance of events, but not their original dimensions.

A woman dressed in white came to me again tonight. She is not welcome here. It's now dawn, and I have been up almost all night.

My eyes seek the sky, the luminous clouds, before sleep. A devout person once wrote, "All is vanity, all is delusion except these infinite heavens."

In the Most Silent of Silences

I can hear my own breathing. As I breathe in, the same high note always plays, like a note from a distant violin, or the hum of a nearby mosquito. As I breathe out, a heavy wagon rolls down a dirt road, a rough country wagon pulled by draft horses of the kind I imagine were used before the automotive age. These sounds accompany my being as persistently as my awareness of the passage of time. The more silent the world, the more clearly I can hear them. In fact, it's these sounds that give me time—its tempo and physiology, its give and take. The air that flows in and out of me is the substance of time—it's time itself.

In girls' school a tall cupboard was brought into the gymnasium once a year. Every girl had to bare their bosom and climb inside. But the eye that illuminated them was not interested in their budding breasts. To that eye, their busts were merely a haze through which it scrutinized the throbbing chambers of their lungs. Each year the same doctor repeated the same demands: "Breathe iii-in! Hooo-old it! You may go!"

The doctor then allowed the girls to let out the time that they had held trapped in their lungs and step out of the temporary prison cell. Even back then, my wagon moved in the dirt of the road, though somewhat more lightly.

I'm already up and have arrived at the office of *The New Anomalist*, though my workday hasn't actually begun yet. I'm tired from my cough, which woke me up early. A cough is a lack of order; it interferes with the rhythm of time. It's January once more, and my umpteenth birthday.

My uncle once wrote in my friend book:

> *Your heart is an empty book*
> *Waiting for each day's fresh-marked page*
> *Your joys, your sorrows, the record of an age*
> *Sights and wonders, the draught of life you took.*
> *The year draws to its close, and January begins anew.*

I feel the irritation on the inner surface of my bronchi, how swollen they are, how red.

In the dark recesses of my chest, alveoli perish one by one. How many are there? How many do I need to be able to live and breathe? How little I know of the ceaseless workings of my insides—a space where thrombocytes float to the beats of my still-hot heart.

As I make some coffee, I watch the winter day break outside the window next to the ceiling. The same life force that passes through my chest is the wind that sways both the empty swing in the playground opposite and the lone, naked tree in the yard. The tree's branches and roots, the branches of my alveoli and vascular system, even river deltas, all organize themselves according to the same laws, follow the same patterns.

I wonder why the swing hasn't been put away for the winter. I wonder at the silent collaboration between my organs and cells that continues without me—the end result of that collaboration—knowing or having to do anything about it. It goes on so that I can sit here underneath the window and watch the wind swirling in the empty yard and wonder why the swing has been left outside for the winter.

The door bell rang just once, and so softly that I doubted my hearing. I opened the door, just to be sure, and there stood a man, neat and shy, belted up in a raincoat. Behind him a curtain of sleet reached all the way to heavens. Mumbling so quietly that I had to strain my ears, he introduced himself and told me he was a subscriber to *The New Anomalist*.

"Since mumblemumblemumble," he whispered.

16

Naturally, I asked him to come in and take off his coat.

"I'm also interested in alternative mumblemumble," he continued after hanging his coat slowly and carefully on the coat rack and arranging himself as meticulously in one of our two kitchen chairs.

His hair was silvery and recently barbered. In his white shirt and elegant dove grey suit, he could have passed for a politician or the CEO of a mid-sized technology company. Perhaps he was one or the other, I never did find out what he did for a living.

"It's a very interesting branch of mumblemumble, if I may say so."

I was cold and had the urge to cough. I longed for another cup of coffee. My wearying dreams had been haunted by dwarfs and boa constrictors.

"I'm sorry, I didn't quite catch what that alternative thing was."

"Audiotechnology," he said.

"I see," I said, without seeing at all.

He looked at me in anticipation and I looked back at him. When I realized he wasn't going to continue, I had to confess: "I can't say that I know what alternative audiotechnology is."

He raised his eyebrows, this well-behaved man in a grey suit. He was the Master of Sound. That is what I call him, and I often find myself reminiscing about him. I've forgotten his real name. He was one of the many acquaintances I made while working as a subeditor of *The New Anomalist*. He was one of the ones—the heretics, the monomaniacs—whose obsessions took up residence in my head.

He said, "Sounds are everywhere, even where you wouldn't think mumblemumble. We don't hear them, but they exist nonetheless. Even in the most silent of silences."

DATURA

When the violin plays—today in pianissimo—I can smell it. A saccharine, almost foul scent exudes from the flower, my birthday present. From its pot, it dominates the room, my gaze, my nose. How heavy and yet translucent the white trumpet-shaped corolla are. How they bend and sway with the slightest touch of a finger.

It arrived with my sister and brother-in-law as a present, but also as a gatecrasher.

"Have you seen this type of flower before? I can't remember what it's called," Noora said as I unwrapped the cellophane surrounding the plant. "Roope hasn't seen it yet either. Maybe you both know what it is. The lady at the flowershop told me its name, but I was in such a rush that I wasn't listening."

"Now that's what I call a shrub!" Roope said.

We appraised the specimen. Its stem was an intense green and its blossoms white as moonlight. Looking at it made me dizzy. The dozen long, trumpet-like flowers reminded me of alabaster jewelry. A few had already withered. I saw the seed pods, round and thorny. I'd never owned such a plant, but one summer, I had admired one in the botanical gardens in another city. There, having wintered inside a greenhouse, it had grown and branched out into a small tree.

"I believe it's an angel's trumpet," I said.

"That's what I think it was! Angel's trumpet! The flowers do look like small trumpets, don't they."

19

"It's a night bloomer," my brother-in-law said. He's an amateur gardener like me, but knows much more about botany. "The flowers open at night. The smell is also stronger during the night. And when spring comes, you can plant it in a sheltered and sunny spot."

"Wonderful. I think I'll take it to the summer house," I said.

"They said at the flowershop that it can't winter this far north, so you'll have to bring it back inside in the autumn."

"I've heard that it's sometimes called devil's weed," Roope said. "Did you know that, Noora?"

"I bought a weed as a gift?" Noora was shocked.

"At least it's related to devil's weed."

Roope rubbed a leaf between his fingers and then sniffed them. He grimaced.

"The smell isn't all that good. Technically it's not a brugmansia, an angel's trumpet, but a datura, a moonflower. The flowers on this one are erect, while those of brugmansia are pendulous. They are sometimes considered the same species, though. It's a datura, I'm pretty sure of it."

"Why do they call it devil's weed?"

"I think datura were once used in witchcraft," Roope said. "It's poisonous. It has intoxicating qualities."

"Oh no, it doesn't seem like a very good birthday present after all," Noora said.

"I like it. It's gorgeous," I said. "We don't have to use it to bewitch anyone."

Another coughing fit came over me and just didn't seem to stop. I went to the kitchen to drink a glass of water, and when I got back, Roope said, "Did you know that this plant is said to cure asthma? Its poison can be used as medicine in small amounts. As is almost always the case with poisons."

"Really? And how are you supposed to take it? Eat fresh flowers? Dry them and smoke them? Use the leaves as tea? Chew ripe seeds?"

"Don't ask me. And don't go trying it out, it might be dangerous. It just came to mind—I remember reading it somewhere. Forget it."

After Roope and Noora had left, I fell asleep for a while. When I woke up, the datura was there, in front of my eyes, like a guardian of my dreams. Dear lord, what a plant! It swelled with vitality, flourishing more by the minute.

Out of impulse, I took one seed pod and crushed it between my fingers. The seeds were black and kidney shaped. I took a mortar and pestle and ground a couple of the seeds to powder. Why not, I thought, just as an experiment. Two seeds was a small amount in my opinion, just the right amount to be used as medicine. And it was a natural remedy after all. I made a sandwich with some sliced tomatoes and sprinkled some sea salt and the seed powder over the top.

I chewed. A strange, completely foreign odor drifted up from the sandwich. A smell that I couldn't link to any other plant. It wasn't a fresh scent like the smell of so many herbs, but musty in some indefinable way. I fought back my revulsion, chewed and swallowed. I was soon overcome by drowsiness. I undressed and went to bed.

The violin screeched; wagon wheels rumbled on a dirt road. I became conscious of these sounds. My mouth felt dry, but I soon fell asleep without much coughing. I had a feeling that I'd last felt as a child at bedtime: it was as though I was riding a spinning merry-go-round with my hair flying in the wind, only I was lying down as it went round and round. I found I still enjoyed it as much as I had as a child.

I only woke once, in the small hours of the night. I felt that someone in a white dress was standing at the foot of the bed. Before I could take fright I realized that it was only the tall moonflower watching over my rest.

Then the merry-go-round started up again, spinning at a dizzying speed.

THE NEW ANOMALIST

The ceiling in the room was so low that even people my height instinctively walked with a slight hunch. The floor was made of unpainted concrete. The radiator was scalding hot from the beginning of September to the end of May, and there was no way to turn it down. Even when I'd bothered to wash the narrow window near the ceiling, the only window in the room, it was just as dusty again after a few days. The window faced northeast and opened onto a narrow asphalt deck where the printing house's employees parked their cars. But at least I was able to see a strip of the opposite building's yard between two brick walls—a swing and a birch tree. The air was not good in the room, which had once been a warehouse for hubcaps. Not a good thing considering the state of my poor lungs.

But that was where *The New Anomalist* was put together.

The chief editor and founder of the magazine was my former class mate Markus, who has been called the Marquis since childhood, probably because everyone at school thought he was strange and a bit snobbish. When the Marquis suggested I become the assistant editor of *The New Anomalist*, I doubted whether I was suitable for the job, because I wasn't familiar with the magazine's subject matter.

"You'll acclimatize soon enough," the Marquis said.

He was right. It wasn't long before I was familiar with anomalies, strange phenomena and the occult, the supernatural and the paranormal, many dissident thoughts and alternative world views. In short, mostly rubbish.

We believe, we secretly hope, that the flux of mysteries would open...

23

Without a doubt *The New Anomalist* sought to sate this eternal appetite in its readers.

Every now and again, amid the marginal, petty, and perhaps even harmful, something noteworthy would pop up, something with some connection to reality and not just delusions inside someone's head. No one ever taught me how to tell them apart. I can only guess that sometimes it's possible to move from the margins and break into the mainstream, from the realm of pseudoscience into respected scientific circles.

The magazine published news and articles on all kinds of paranormal phenomena, extrasensory perception, magic and the occult, millennialism, catastrophism, prophesies, astral traveling, demonology, cryptozoology, channeling, remote viewing, chiropractic, holism, the holographic paradigm, kundalini, reiki and shamanism, numerology, past life regression therapy, black helicopters, MKULTRA documents, the Illuminati, spontaneous human combustion, the goth subculture, as well as poltergeists, ghosts, and apparitions, just to name a few.

The Q&A column would deal with how to make a psychotronic generator or how to take Kirlian photos at home or what reference works had the best information on the basics of alchemy, martinism, or chaos magic. Every now and then we also published news on apparitions and miracles, stigma and bleeding statues.

However, the Marquis didn't want to feature anything that had to do with spiritism, psychic surgery, spiritual healing, or ufology. It was a difficult, sometimes even impossible, distinction to make.

We also had a paranoia section, a paraphysics section, and pages for parapsychology and parabiology. The paranoia section covered alleged government cover-ups, scheming authorities, and international conspiracies. Paraphysics and alternative technology took up a few spreads. The columns on those pages would introduce the reader to alternatives to the theory of relativity, free energy, time travel, antimatter, cold fusion, and cryonics.

The parapsychology section would have features on things like orgonomy and transpersonal psychology. The parabiology section focused on alternative evolution theories—of which there are many, believe me—cryptids, the aquatic ape hypothesis, and exobiology.

Sometimes we got messages from "Otherkin," people who didn't think they were humans, but other forms of life.

The number of subscribers doubled within just a few years, but the editor and the assistant editor still had to do everything ourselves.

As time went by, the Marquis turned more and more tasks over to his subeditor, meaning, me. My inbox would have dozens of new messages every morning, and my desk would be covered with random material, both letters from readers and newspaper articles in English, French, and German.

I became an expert on concepts like "vibrational frequency," "bioenergy," and "energy field." Many of the terms had been appropriated from theoretical physics or information technology. I learned what kind of creatures the Nguoi Rungs were and that ectoplasm was a slimy, disgusting looking substance that would gush from the ears and mouths of turn-of-the-century mediums.

The Marquis seldom came to the office, but I had to spend nearly six hours a day in that rathole. I tried to make it a bit more cozy. I put a rug on the concrete floor and brought in an armchair with torn corduroy upholstery that I'd found at a flea market. By throwing a blanket over the armchair, I managed to make it look neat and welcoming. I put a table lamp with a green lampshade on my desk and even put a light therapy lamp on the windowsill. I grew a couple of Phalaenopsis orchids in its glow.

My first *Anomalist* winter was especially dark. There was no snow, only icy drizzle. Still, I must confess that even then I liked the midwinter, even if it was snowless, the bleakest time imaginable. The dead of winter is like a pocket you can hide in. Winter offers one of the best illusions: the illusion that time can stop. If nothing grows, blooms, or flourishes, nothing can wither away, either.

The city in winter is more present and real than during other seasons. The lights of windows, cars, shops, and theaters, all of them speak of presence, that there are others like me. When the lights fade as the sun climbs higher, when the growing season begins and summer finally comes, I almost forget about people. I concentrate on the world of vegetation, the vibrant life of sprouts, shoots, and buds.

But there, back then, the short days repeated as if they were one and the same day, and we, too, repeated the day before again and again.

> "Old clouds never clear
> Dawn breaks with them lowering.
> And each new day here
> its own verse neverending."

We lived in the eternity of winter, thinking we would always remain the same, trying not to see what was changing.

The Master of Sound

"Sounds are everywhere, even where you wouldn't think mumble-mumble. We don't hear them, but they exist. Even in the most silent of silences."

The lowering silver sky, the Master of Sound's suit, and his muted voice were all of one color.

"I'm sorry, but could you explain this alternative audiotechnology a bit more," I said, slightly impatiently. "I've only worked here a few weeks. There are so many important topics in this field that I've never heard of before."

"Alternative audiotechnology is a means to reveal sounds that the human ear usually can't mumblemumble," the Master of Sound explained in a friendly, but extremely quiet voice.

I was annoyed. I felt like I would have needed alternative audiotechnology just to be able to hear what this man had to say.

"Everyday life would be quite chaotic, though, if we could hear every single noise," I said. "I'd think the fact that the human ear can hear only as much as it does is practical, lucky even."

"The brain's task is, of course, to mumblemumble," he concurred. "The brain cannot take in everything. But the mumblemumblemumble of our hearing leads us to believe that there is nothing else to be heard. The same goes with all our senses, even mumblemumblemumble".

His voice became so quiet again that I had to concentrate. "I'm sorry, I didn't quite catch that."

"Even our intellect and knowledge," he repeated. "We cannot begin to know what we don't know! We can't even begin to guess!"

"You're right about that," I said. It was actually a completely new idea to me despite its simplicity.

"And still we are so convinced that we know something substantial mumblemumble mum mumble mum."

"Pardon me?" He was really starting to get on my nerves.

"Something substantial about the laws and regularities of the universe," he said.

"Don't we, then?"

"A little of this and that, without a doubt. But reality isn't limited to the world we know. And sometimes we should mumblemumble or at least mumblemumble to hear a bit more than we normally hear," he continued. "It does wonders to broaden one's mumble. That's why I've created a mumblemumble mumble.

"Excuse me?"

"A Detector of Silent Sounds."

"What's that?" I asked.

"A very simple device," he said. " I have a tape recorder that is activated by even the weakest of sounds. I leave it in an empty room, when I go to work. No one else has a mumble to the room."

"I beg your pardon?"

"No one else has a key to the room. Last year I had the walls mumblemumble. When I get back from work, I listen to the tape."

"Every day?"

"Every day. It's become a mumblemumble."

"I'm sorry?"

"A habit. But, naturally, there isn't always anything to listen to."

"Are you saying that there are times when you've heard something peculiar? Sounds in an empty and locked room?"

"Certainly, many times. Sometimes I've heard a buzz as if from a mumble nest. Other times it sounds like some mumblemumblemumblemumble."

"Excuse me?

"Like some vehicle is accelerating and decelerating."

"I see," I said. "Hmm. Very interesting. Would you perhaps consider writing an article for *The New Anomalist* about this phenomenon?"

"Why not?" said the Master of Sound. "That's what I had in mind.

But there is no reason to mumblemum only on this phenomenon. Alternative mumblemumble, of course, has so much more to offer. It can reveal to us totally mumblemumble things about the universe and human life."

"Is that so?"

"Maybe you've heard of instrumental mumblemumblemumble?"

"Pardon me?"

"Instrumental transcommunication."

"I must say I haven't."

"Or of Doctor Konstantin Raudive and his mumblemumble."

"Excuse me"

"Of his goniometer."

"No, unfortunately not."

He looked displeased.

"Well, maybe you've heard of EVP, then?"

"I'm not familiar with that either," I said, already embarrassed at the gap in my education.

"EVP stands for electronic voice phenomenon," he explained patiently.

"I seem to learn something new every day in this job."

"EVP sounds typically last only a mumble or two and can barely be heard. Usually you must use good mumblemumble and train your mumble to be able to distinguish them."

I stopped listening to him at some point, I was so tired and annoyed. It was hard having to constantly strain my hearing, although what he was talking about was strange and new to me, and interesting in that sense, at least.

"Very well," I said, rudely interrupting his mumbling at long last. "Excellent. Write a short article about this subject for us. Of course, I can't guarantee it will be published. Let's aim for the next issue. Your deadline is at the beginning of March."

"Mumblemumble!" he uttered, seemingly pleased. "Goodbye. Mumblemumblemumble!"

"Excuse me?"

"It was nice to meet you," whispered the Master of Sound, disappearing silently into the pale winter's day.

THE VOYNICH MANUSCRIPT

My cough was no longer as hacking and tormenting as before. I didn't need my inhaler anymore. Each night I ate a tomato sandwich with a few datura seeds on top or drank tea made from datura leaves. There were some side effects, though. I had to drink much more than normal, because datura was dehydrating. That's why it worked well as cough medicine.

At times I also had some difficulty focusing my eyes. When I glanced in the mirror, I saw that my pupils were large and unusually glassy. In that way, datura had a similar effect to belladonna. It made my eyes beautiful.

A facsimile edition of an ancient manuscript had appeared on the corner table. The Marquis had also brought me various articles in French and Latin that he said were attempts to interpret the manuscript. I didn't know what he expected me to do with them. I only knew basic Latin and my French wasn't very good either. I didn't recognize the language of the manuscript or even the alphabet. I reckoned, however, that it might have been Romanic or Arabic. The hand was skilled and beautiful; there were no corrections to be seen.

I flipped through the manuscript, getting more intrigued by the minute. It looked medieval and was richly illuminated: symbols, maps, circles, celestial bodies or maybe cells, it was impossible to know. Naked women with rosy cheeks bathing, and animals of unknown species, possibly frogs, salamanders, fish, cats, lions…

The colorful etchings, which depicted odd flowers and herbs, appealed to me the most. Some of them looked like they were connected to man-made components, maybe tubes or cables. Or were they snakes? Some of the imaginary plants had been linked together into some kind of dancing line.

Human faces were everywhere, in astronomical pictures as well as hidden in the leaves and roots of plants.

"What is this?" I asked the Marquis.

"It's the Voynich manuscript."

"Who's Voynich?"

"Voynich was the name of the American book dealer who found the manuscript in a Jesuit monastery in Frascati at the turn of the last century, though it's been suspected that Voynich himself was the author. He believed that it was written by Doctor Mirabilis, Roger Bacon. The real origin of the manuscript is still unknown. No one knows where or when it was written or who wrote it. But usually it's dated to the fifteenth century at the earliest."

"This language…"

"This is the only known example of the language. But it seems to contain elements from various languages. It might be a cipher, some dead language, or some sort of ancient artificial language. Many cryptologists have tried to decipher it for almost a hundred years now, and there are many transcriptions. Yet no one has been able to interpret the manuscript."

I was surprised that the Marquis was so enthusiastic about the book and knew so much about it.

"The alphabet doesn't resemble any European writing system. Yet it supposedly originates in Europe, although the words are shorter than in Latin, English, German, or French. Not to mention the Scandinavian languages."

"The handwriting is beautiful," I said.

"But notice," he said, "that it's written in two different hands. The writers were highly educated and skillful, they didn't make any corrections to the text. But it doesn't seem to be just a matter of different handwriting, but of different languages or at least different dialects. There is a great deal of repetition in both of them, the entropy of the text, as they say, is very low."

The Marquis seemed pleased to be able to surprise me with his expertise. "So what does that mean?"

"It means that the text could be written in some code; it's a combination of numbers and various symbols. One researcher tried to argue that each character is composed of up to twenty strokes, each of which he thought could have been an individual letter. That theory hasn't gotten much support. It's possible that the Voynich manuscript is some kind of encyclopedia. It also could be that the language doesn't exist at all, that it's just nonsense, a practical joke, a hoax."

"These plants…"

"They say that even botanists can't identify the species. I want you to write a short essay on the Voynich manuscript."

I enjoy looking at and flipping through this book. I've already read many articles about it and started my own. For some reason, though, it's stalled, I can't get past the introduction.

The Voynich manuscript is an odd book, but then again, all books are odd. Often when I leaf through this manuscript or even when I happen to just lay my eyes on it, I'm astonished. Many times I've found myself thinking of writing in general, books, their meaning, the way in which they exist. I ask myself what writing actually is. How the personal changes into the public, and why it must be so.

There are moments when everything is new, as if seen or heard for the first time, even language, words that I've read a thousand times. People, landscapes, items, even books. Now and then I stop at a familiar word as I read, and all of a sudden it amazes me, and I savour it like a new taste. For a fraction of a second I hesitate: what does the word refer to, does it really signify anything at all?

In those moments, I'm like a newborn. I see the world like I once saw a flower that had been picked from the garden and placed in a vase. I wake up as if from another dream and look around myself for the first time. At times like that, all books are like the Voynich manuscript to me: ciphers, cryptographies, beyond all interpretation.

MINERAL, PLANT, OR
ANIMAL KINGDOM?

"Soul? What are they talking about?" the Marquis once asked. "What's that supposed to be? Give me a hint. Does it belong to the mineral, plant, or animal kingdom?"

What a cynical person. And this man, this extreme rationalist, was the editor of *The New Anomalist*! There was something almost immoral about it.

The Marquis secretly made fun of the magazine's readers, but their money, *that* he was more than happy to take.

"I founded the *The New Anomalist* because there was a demand for this kind of magazine. Because I reckoned that sooner or later it would become a success. I had no so-called ideological motives, purely commercial ones. Why should I believe in the garbage that gets published in *The New Anomalist*? I'm a sane, mature, rational, and well-read person," he said. "I firmly believe in the ability of science to explain the world around us."

"You think that the world has been designed by some kind of project development manager," I said.

I disapproved of his attitude towards editing the magazine, though I wasn't sure that mine was any more honorable.

"You don't see an ethical problem here?" I asked. "Can a vegetarian open a steak house?" I asked. "For you to publish *The New Anomalist* is just as strange."

"I think the question you should ask is can a meat eater open a vegetarian restaurant? And my answer is: why on earth not? If I don't

35

do it, someone else would publish this magazine," and probably do a much worse job."

"That's one argument," I said, "but not a good one."

As I examined my own relationship to the magazine and its endless anomalies, I had to confess that it, too, was problematic. As the Marquis once remarked, I flirted with the so-called paranormal. I evaded, denied, rejected, and laughed at it, and then was drawn towards it again.

"Do you believe that one day science could explain the ultimate secrets of existence?" I once asked him.

"Of course not," he said, "because no such secrets exists."

"Tell me then, what do you believe in?" I insisted.

The Marquis fell silent for a while, and then gave the following speech. It was clear and, for him, so well-put that I suspected he had read it somewhere. The Marquis had a good memory. For that I'm grateful to him.

"I believe, as I assume you also believe, that the universe was created by chance—pure, free, blind chance. I believe that it's lifeless, that it has no meaning or creator. I believe that organic life, not to mention human life, is a unique exception in the universe. Neither have any meaning in or to the universe. The universe doesn't see us, hear us, know anything about us, or care one bit about our thoughts and hopes. In all probability, humans represent the highest form of intelligent life in the universe.

"Reality can be observed through senses or instruments. Humans suffer the same ultimate fate as all flesh, because we are our bodies and nothing more. Heredity and environment define us completely. Intellect is a by-product of physical energy.

"I believe that only humans are conscious. Falling in love, religious and ecstatic experiences, prophecies and visions, are all dysfunctions of the brain when the intellect momentarily loses control. There is no consciousness without brain activity. Death is, therefore, the inexorable end of the intellect and the so-called soul."

There it was, the Marquis's credo. Yet despite his ultra-rationalism he carries amulets with him, which makes me question his commitment to his declared world view. Once a pendant with some kind of hieroglyph engraved on it fell from his pocket.

"What's this?" I asked, as I picked it up. "Is it yours?"

"What does it matter?" he said childishly and put it back in his pocket.

I came across the same symbol by accident, as I was checking an article sent to us about Egyptian cosmology. I learned that it stood for khu, the human soul.

THE QUIET ASPHALT

That morning I felt so bad that I almost couldn't get out of bed. It wasn't the asthma. My symptoms were milder than they often were in the spring, and I believed it was because of the datura. But now my eyes were sensitive to light, my head hurt, my mouth was dry, and my heart was pounding. I thought I might be suffering some sort of migraine, an experience I hadn't had before. There was another possibility, but I refused to even consider it.

It wasn't until the afternoon that I dragged my aching body to the office. As a result, I ended up sitting there late into the night answering emails and reading a transcription of the Voynich manuscript:

POGR. G. SOE. TOEOR. PZOE.
TOR. TB2. TOPTOE. OHCCA.

I was left none the wiser.

The thaw had come, and snow had changed to rain. I watched the raindrops that rolled down the window every now and again. It's a pastime, a cheap amusement, that I've been fond of since childhood. Some raindrops seem to hesitate and slow down; others are more hasty and immediately go their solitary way, but many come together to form broad streams. All raindrops seek their own path, as if each had its own will and personality and future, some other option than just falling from the eaves into a puddle. In my basement hole in the wall, I contemplated whether it was possible that each of them had their own soul, which was born when they separated from the cloud and died when they joined the earth's waterways.

I fell asleep in the armchair for a while, comforted by the sound of rain. I woke a couple of times thinking that someone had turned on the light or that maybe there had been a flash of lightning. I'd had the same experience many nights now, and I had started to wonder whether there really was something wrong with my eyes. Only the reading lamp with a green lamp shade shone on my desk and I didn't hear any thunder. I drifted off once more.

As I woke, I felt more healthy and alert. I had slept into the early morning hours and the rain had stopped. Buses and trams didn't run at this hour and I didn't have money for a cab. With the weather having improved, I decided to walk home and take in the mild night air.

There was still life at the hotdog and taxi stands. A final few bursts of revellers erupted from the bars and restaurants. Here and there, I could hear drunken brawling and fits of laughter. Some nutcase was walking unsteadily along the tram rails screaming abuse at an invisible antagonist. There was hardly any traffic, but every once in a while a cab would speed by. I took a longer route home, walking swiftly. I didn't want to walk through the park alone at night.

As I reached the footbridge, I stopped, even though I was feeling a bit cold. I stood and gazed at the pastel dawn spreading across the horizon. Under the bridge ran a beltway, glistening black from the rain. I'd never seen it this empty. I'd read somewhere that a type of quiet asphalt was being tested around this area, a compound that would lessen the sounds of car tires. From the east, where the dawn was beginning to turn to daylight, a silent column of cars was approaching.

For some reason I waited for them to pass under the bridge. I leaned on the railing under the brightening sky and watched the advancing convoy. It moved toward the bridge in a long line. I started to feel nervous, but didn't understand why right away. The vehicles were new and shiny, all the same color, metallic gray. They were a strange and unusual shape, elongated somehow, and I couldn't recognize the make.

The cars moved remarkably steadily. I estimated that they were travelling 50 miles per hour, which was the speed limit. But there was something odd about this procession, something frightening. The cars were driving just a few yards apart. Far too close to one another at that speed, and on a wet road no less. The drivers must have been extremely skilled, because as I followed their progress, the distances between all the cars seemed to remain the same down to an inch. It was as if they had been linked together like rail cars, only with invisible connectors.

From my vantage point I could watch the cars' procession for a good while before they reached the bridge. I watched them the whole way, forgetting my weariness and even where I was, because there was something magical about the cars' movement. A moment before they reached me, I noticed something that nearly made my knees go weak, nearly made me sick. I grabbed the railing with both hands.

The windshield of the first car was clean and clear. I could clearly see the steering wheel, even the pattern of the fabric on the driver's seat—geometric figures, green-tinted spirals on a blue background— the harsh halogen lights of the bridge revealed the inside of the car. I couldn't see a driver. I couldn't see a single soul in the car. No one was driving the vehicle. That's what I saw, no driver, not even a single passenger. It moved along empty and shining and new. I looked at the next vehicle and the front seat was also empty. Then came the third, the fourth. All empty.

I was consumed with fear. My diaphragm stiffened. I asked myself whether hallucinations can also be negative: that you don't see things that are, that must be, there. There was the possibility that the cars themselves were a delusion, but I refused to believe it, I had seen the details of each car so clearly and felt the gusts of dispersed air as they drove by.

I searched for some passerby, anyone, an eyewitness, who could tell me that what I saw was real—or not. I was afraid of both alternatives, but I didn't know which one scared me more. If the witness didn't see what I saw—or more precisely, saw what I didn't see—I'd think I'd lost my mind. If the witness saw the same thing I did—an empty line of shining cars—then, so I thought, the world would be even more strange than I'd ever believed.

No one came, no one passed by. I wouldn't have had time to look for a witness at any rate, as the last phantom car of the procession had already passed under the bridge. I saw the shining line disappear humming into the distance like some mechanical worm. The separate vehicles seemed to have flowed into each other organically and irrevocably.

But where were the people? Where had they been left behind?

Those perfect machines glistening in the sunrise seemed to me to be racing toward the future, where humans no longer had any role to play, not as drivers, not even as passengers. And before the hard light of the day eclipsed the colors of sunrise, the cars sped up, and their wheels seemed to lift off the dirty road, and they flew over the quiet asphalt like phantoms of the new millennium.

THE PARASTORE

My state of mind and health fluctuated violently that year. There were days when I wandered around in a state of agitation from morning until night and it was hard for me to sit still and concentrate on anything. I was constantly thirsty and always carried a water bottle that I had to refill several times a day. I felt that I was full of a new and different kind of energy. I'd be tempted to say *alternative* if that hadn't become such a worn-out word.

And then there were days when I was washed out, I felt ancient and I could sleep for fourteen hours straight without stirring. I also suffered from anxiety attacks and dizzy spells. That had never happened before. At night my eyes would sometimes snap wide open. It was as though someone had switched on the light, even though it was pitch black.

On one such day of weariness, as the winter air pushed sleet and the smell of exhaust fumes into the office, someone knocked on the door.

"I have an idea," the Marquis said.

"Really?" I said cautiously.

"Let's open up a store, a parastore!"

"In here?"

"Don't look so shocked. It could be a mail-order service. It could have all sorts of things that people could order by email, things relating to the magazine's profile, stuff that would interest our readers."

"Such as?"

"Well, you know, healing crystals, floral scent remedies, tarot cards, magnets, amulets, ouija boards…"

43

I started to get angry. "Oh, I know, believe me. Worthless junk that silly teenagers spend their allowances on. Don't even think of trying to make me run the store."

"Don't kill my idea right off the bat. Take it easy. Just consider it. The store might become a success."

"Physical objects don't move from place to place digitally. Tell me, where are we going to fit everything? And who do you think is going to handle the orders, and pack and mail them?"

The Marquis looked at me with raised eyebrows.

"Not under any circumstances. I refuse, completely. I came to work here as a subeditor, not as some door-to-door salesman."

"Nothing cheers people up in hard times like this kind of junk," the Marquis said, dreamily. "Take a look at this. This could be one sales item. It falls into the goth subculture, I'd say."

He handed me a small box. I opened it and saw a phosphorescent miniature skeleton.

The shop was set up, as had been clear it would from the start. Not even a month went by before I was unpacking parcels. The Marquis had ordered merchandise all the way from China, India, and the United States. With great displeasure I rooted around in styrofoam peanuts for small aromatherapy vials, crystal balls, healing stones, Tibetan chimes, yin-yang pendants, T-shirts with pictures of the Chupacabra, the Sphinx, and werewolves. Amethysts and rose quartz. Small glass pyramids. Scented candles, essential oils, herbal tea. Ritualistic items, African amulets, and sharks' teeth. Chinese doormats with dragon designs. Those I liked, and I took the liberty of putting one by the door to the office.

A whole fortune was invested in this eclectic collection of items, and I was afraid that if they didn't sell *The New Anomalist*—and me with it—would be driven into financial ruin.

Products could be ordered by email or bought directly from our office, although I fought that to the last. My territory was reduced by half, with the parastore taking up the other half. Officially it was only open on Thursday and Friday afternoons, but in practice the doorbell would ring on any day of the week and in would walk someone who just had to have a shark's tooth or a skeleton puzzle or a fake crystal. And I obliged, what else could I have done?

One day the Marquis swept in and put a sign on the counter: IN GOD WE TRUST. EVERYONE ELSE PAYS CASH. He thought it was funny, so it was there to stay.

He also gave me a new task. "How about you write an article about the death of Countess Cornelia di Bandi for our next issue."

"Who?" I asked. "I've never heard of her. Not local, I presume."

"No," he said. "Check it out online. Spontaneous human combustion. We haven't had anything on the subject for a long time. The countess died in 1731, as far as I can remember. I need the article by Monday. Three hundred words will be fine."

I looked the case up. It really wasn't news anymore, even Charles Dickens had written about it. The countess's chamber maid had found the remains of Cornelia di Bandi in the countess's bedroom. Not much left. Only her disembodied feet were left lying on the floor with her head between them. The rest of her body had burned down to a small pile of ash, but the room was otherwise untouched.

Since for whatever reason the Marquis thought it was necessary, I started to write a short account of the countess and her wretched fate. But I also had an article on the early life of Nicola Tesla to finish.

THE DAY OF THE PLUM PUDDING

"Did you know that a few years back two men with the same name disappeared on the same day in this city?" Mr. Chance asked me on one exceptionally windy day. He, too, was one of my acquaintances, one of the Heretics. Mr. Chance had already retired, and he had time to stop by our office a couple of times a week to blabber about his favorite topics.

He was fixated on coincidence. It was his monomania. No matter what the topic of discussion originally was, whenever he was there, sooner or later the discussion would turn to coincidence. He couldn't stop wondering at the secret order of nature, the principle of non-causal connection, which according to Mr. Chance was a background influence on all linear events. According to him, this universal principle manifested itself in coincidences, events that he liked to call serial and that in his opinion were connected through the experience of meaningfulness. He liked to emphasize that synchronism and seriality could not be explained by the known laws of nature, and therefore, our view of the world was not only incomplete, but flawed.

Technically he was still a graduate student. He hadn't finished his master's thesis in political science before being completely swept away by the non-academic study of coincidences. He had earned his living for forty years as a janitor at a data center. During that time he had accumulated a collection of composition notebooks, in which he'd recorded all the coincidences he'd noticed each day, as well as where and when they took place. His inspiration for this beloved hobby was

47

probably the biologist Paul Kammerer, a scientist he worshipped and often talked about.

"Kammerer was the man," Mr. Chace enlightened me, "who was destroyed by midwife toads. He was the researcher who thought that he could use the toads to prove that characteristics acquired during the lifetime of one specimen could be passed on to its offspring. His research results—or at least some of them—were exposed as fabrications. It killed him. But no one really knows who was actually responsible for the fabrication. I trust in Kammerer's honesty.

"I sometimes think," Mr. Chance continued shyly, "that Paul Kammerer would value my humble notes to some degree. He himself recorded one of the most extensive and important collections of coincidences at the beginning of the twentieth century."

"I'm certain that he would have been interested in your observations," I said. "How did he gather his material?"

"He always had a notebook at hand and constantly wrote things down, whether he was sitting on a park bench or on a train or waiting for his meal in a restaurant. He classified the people he saw according to their age, clothing, and gender, and he even made notes about what they were carrying in their hands. He compiled statistics on the basis of his data and noticed to his surprise that many of the parameters cumulated in time."

On the day that I always remember as the Day of the Plum Pudding, Mr. Chance insisted that we leave the stuffy office and go for a small walk by the sea. A bracing northwestern wind, he claimed, would stimulate the mind and body.

As soon as I opened the door, a chill winter wind grabbed at my scarf. I wrapped it around my neck twice over. The bay had not yet frozen, and the last boat of the year struggled to make headway, disappearing at times behind waves hemmed with white caps.

"What was that story about the two men with the same name?" I asked him.

"A true story," Mr. Chance said emphatically. "They had the same first, middle, and last names. But they weren't related and didn't even know each other—nor are the reasons that led to their disappearances connected at all."

"Were they ever found?" I asked him.

"How about we sit here?" Mr. Chance said, pointing to a damp bench under an oak that had already shed its leaves. What a marvelous tree! The ancient vitality of its black roots had spread its canopy over two paths in the park. A cloud swept over the tree's crown as if one of the waving branches had chased it away.

"One of them was found in 'the Cholera basin,' the harbor basin in front of the market square. I've heard nothing about the fate of the other man."

"That certainly is an curious case. But what does that prove?" I asked him. "Things like that happen, why wouldn't they? There is so much happening in the world every minute that it would hardly be possible to avoid bizarre coincidences."

Mr. Chance continued on without paying my question any heed. He told me that very recently, in a small town on the western coast (I can't remember where exactly), the young driver of a Mazda 323 lost control of the car in a left-hand curve, and went off the road. The car was wrecked. The driver and four passengers were all injured. Half an hour later at a different left-hand curve in the same town, another young driver of a Mazda 323 lost control of the car, running off road. The car was wrecked. The driver and four passengers were all injured.

"What are the odds of something like that happening?" Mr. Chance asked and pointed his index finger at me.

"Probably not very good," I said. "But sometimes extremely unlikely things do happen. Why wouldn't they?"

"That's not good enough," he said, shaking his head. "Not good enough at all."

Right then a Mazda 323 passed us on the boulevard at walking speed. Mr. Chance didn't seem to notice the car, and I didn't say a word.

"On a different note, you have heard the story of the plum pudding, haven't you?" Mr. Chance asked.

For a moment I thought that he really was going to change the subject, but then he went on, "It's also a true story, well known by aficionados."

I hadn't heard the story, but I was sure that I soon would. I was getting cold, but Mr. Chance didn't even seem to notice the vicious wind. Coincidences kept him in a state of constant agitation to the point that he hardly ever noticed extraneous circumstances.

"Well, when a certain Monsieur Deschamps was a child, he got some plum pudding from a Monsieur de Fortgibu. Where was this again? I can't remember whether it was in the city of Joan of Arc's victory, Orléans, or in Rouen, where she was burned. In any case, years later in a Parisian restaurant, Monsieur Deschamps noticed plum pudding on the menu and got a craving to have some. But when he ordered plum pudding for dessert, the waiter told him that the last of it had just been ordered. As it happens, it had been ordered by the very same Monsieur de Fortgibu."

"That certainly is a coincidence," I said wearily. My eyes searched for the boat, but I couldn't find it anymore. It had perhaps already sailed behind a small islet.

"That's what people tend to say. But listen to this," he insisted. "Years passed, many years, and again Monsieur Deschamps had an incident with plum pudding. He was invited to a party where the kind of pudding in question was being served. While he was eating it, Monsieur Deschamps made a remark to the party that all that was missing was Monsieur de Fortgibu. Right at that moment, the door opened and who walked in but Monsieur Fortgibu himself, already a man of very advanced years, who had meant to go somewhere else entirely. He'd gotten the wrong address, and accidentally gatecrashed the party that Monsieur Deschamps was attending. What do you say to that?"

"Nothing, to be on the safe side," I replied kindly.

The boat was closer than I thought. It was already turning toward the harbor. Now I could see that, although it was a small boat, it had been given a name. "Joan of Arc" was painted on its hull. An unusual name for a boat.

"That might be for the best," Mr. Chance said. "The case of the plum pudding would put anyone at a loss for words. Force them to face a universal enigma. Shall we have a walk in the botanical garden?"

We walked. We sat down again on a bench as damp as the previous one, but more shielded from the lash of the arctic wind. Young and delicate trees, maybe fruit-bearing trees, grew behind the bench. Each one had a nameplate in front of it.

"Do you know what I think? In a way, the universe is like a pudding or maybe Jell-O. Some philosopher has said that before me, though."

"Really?"

"The connection between everything, you see? Things aren't all unrelated, the world isn't a pile of unconnected things. Jell-O trembles, no matter where you poke it with your spoon, the whole thing. Interaction, sameness, oneness, homogeneity… You know what the most important thing in a pudding is?"

"The most important thing? I, for one, judge pudding by its flavor."

I was beginning to lose interest, and by now wanted to go back to the musty warmth of the basement. I heard a bat hit a ball in the sports field, but it was out of sight.

"Precisely! You said it! The most important thing in a pudding is its flavor. And pudding has just one and the same flavor no matter where you stick your spoon in."

I must have looked confused. He lifted his finger and continued, "Here's an analogy for you: pudding—taste! World—meaning! You do understand, don't you?"

"I suppose," I said, with hesitation. "But I have to get back to the office."

"One of these days," Mr. Chance said, "I'll come by your office again. We need to discuss this subject again and dig a bit deeper."

"Without a doubt," I said.

As we got up—I was already chilled to the bone—I happened to take a look at the young fruit tree under which we'd sat. It wasn't an apple tree as I'd assumed, nor a cherry tree. I bent down and read the nameplate.

You got it! *Prunus domestica*, the plate read, a plum tree.

Another Man with the Same Name

Although the circulation of *The New Anomalist* continued to increase, I was unpleasantly aware that the magazine itself wasn't improving. If anything, it was degenerating. The Marquis searched more and more eagerly for sensational material in an effort to increase the magazine's circulation.

He didn't even come to the office every week. But when he did, he'd hum golden oldies or hymns. On good days he'd address me using the names of his favorite songs, "Lalaika" or "Lazzarella." On bad ones, just by my last name. I didn't care for either practice.

He'd stop humming, knock on the door even if it was open, and say, "I have an idea."

And he always did. Unfortunately, his ideas weren't always good. Sometimes they were just awful, and it wasn't unusual for us to end up having a fight. And there were days when I had to put the worst of his ideas into practice as best I could.

The Marquis complained about how *The New Anomalist* took up all his time, but that wasn't really true. I didn't know exactly what he did all day long. Maybe it was true that he sat in the library all day gathering material, as he so readily insisted. Usually, however, he sat in a shady little dive called The Foxhole, which was generally considered a meeting place for the neighborhood's petty criminals. What attracted a man like him to that kind of place will forever be a mystery to me, and maybe it's better that way.

The New Anomalist did take up all of my time, though. The Marquis didn't hesitate to call me during my free time, and he often got his brilliant ideas at night.

If the phone rang at quarter past midnight, I knew who was on the other end of the line.

"Listen up, Lalaika, we need to offer psychic guidance, understand?" I heard after a rude awakening.

"We! Go ahead and say what you really mean. You're planning to force me to become some sort of dial-up psychic..."

"No, no, you're right, you might not suitable for the job. You probably don't have the empathy for it."

"That's rich coming from you!"

"I have a couple of candidates. You can interview them and pick one. 'Ask a Clairvoyant,' now there's an idea! Or maybe, 'Sibyl Says.' Or what about this: 'Write to the Dead!' We can help you communicate with your loved ones beyond the veil. 'Hello from Heaven,' that sort of thing..."

"Now you've gone too far," I said. "Goodnight."

I could never anticipate when the Marquis would show up. Whenever he did come to the office, he'd stay for an hour or at most two, sitting at his computer, and then he'd disappear again. Most of the time he sat surfing through webzines looking for news that would fit our needs.

"Listen to this," the Marquis said, staring at the monitor. I thought how he'd lately become pale and aged. He was probably thinking the same about me.

"Good lord. Here's our 'Rumor of the Month.' "

"What is it?"

"Jesus didn't die at Golgotha. The man who was crucified was his cousin. Jesus himself escaped to Siberia. From there he went on to Japan, where he started a family in his old age."

"No! I refuse to put that in the magazine. Under no circumstances will I agree to that."

"Why on earth not?"

"Do you want to get sued again? That's not the rumor of the month—more like the rumor of the millennium. It might offend someone's religious beliefs, or more likely many people's. I'm tired of replying to angry letters from the readers."

"Fine. How about this, then: the works of Shakespeare weren't written by Shakespeare, but by another man with the same name."

"I suppose that's the better of the two," I said reluctantly.

The things one has to do!

ON AIR, ON SUNLIGHT

Oh, the wisdom of orchids, letting their flowers bloom at the exact moment when there are insects ready to pollinate them! So it is in nature, but down in our basement office, there wasn't a single insect, not one winter fly woken from its hibernation. And yet, my Phalaenopsis orchid was in bloom when I met the Ethnobotanist, the man who had written an article on plant sentience for *The New Anomalist*.

Purple and blue veins intertwined in the white corollas of the Phalaenopsis like a map of the rivers and roads of an unknown country. It was made up of the most ethereal of substances, finer than the finest silk. I felt pride when the Ethnobotanist admired the orchid's inflorescence, as if I myself had caused it.

As I listened to the Ethnobotanist, I recalled some lines from *Spoon River*.

> "My thanks, friends of the
> County Scientific Association,
> Twice I tried to join your honored body,
> And was rejected
> And when my little brochure
> On the intelligence of plants
> Began to attract attention
> You almost voted me in…"

I call him the Ethnobotanist, though he had made an academic career studying lichens. He had then moved on to unorthodox research topics, ethnobotanics, and the psychology of plants. I enjoyed listening to him—he was so enthusiastic, spoke so passionately about things that were so different from what the chief editor of *The New Anomalist* was interested in. I wrote down just some of his thoughts.

"For one thing," he said, "I hope you understand that plants, too, are conscious. The consciousness of plants resembles human dreaming. That, too, is consciousness. Everywhere in the universe, there is consciousness. It is senseless reason that seeks to set humans apart.

"We are convinced that having a brain is an indispensable precondition for intelligence. Not true at all! Intelligence, memory, mind, and spirit run through all flora and fauna, all the way down to single-celled organisms. Where there's life, there's consciousness. It is different for every species and differs at each stage of a plant's life. Woody and herbaceous plants, naturally, have very different ways of thinking and viewing the world. There are many plants, such as tomatoes, that are unusually aware of their environment and are more easily disturbed by human touch.

"Isn't it odd," the Ethnobotanist continued, "that when humans perceive their environment and react appropriately to its changes, we call it intelligence. But when other animals, let alone plants, act the same way, we no longer call it intelligence, but instinct, which we consider inferior. We think that reason, *ratio*, guides our actions. But it does very little of that, which is perhaps a lucky thing. No, it is what we do not feel, what we know nothing about, that also guides us.

"Plants don't change their location nor do they speak the same way as we do. Is that what makes us think of them as them idiots? They move upward, towards the light. That's what we, too, should be doing. The dialogue that plants have with the air and the sun is the foundation of our lives. When will we remember, when will we acknowledge, that our lives are completely and entirely dependent on and at the mercy of plants?

"Plants have conversations with other individuals and even other species, but in their own ways, such as through chemical signals. Did you know that trees have a tremendously keen sense of smell?" the Ethnobotanist asked. "They know when the larva of a pest insect are crawling on their leaves. They start taking specific counter-measures, each according to its species. They even communicate and scheme with other species in order to banish the saboteurs. Security specialists could learn a lot from the alarm systems of plants.

"Perhaps you remember a Dr. Singh? He studied the effect of music on the growth of plants."

"His name sounds familiar," I said. "Wasn't it his research team that made the observation that jazz and classical music accelerated growth, whereas heavy metal slowed it down?"

"He's the one. Many researchers since then have continued his line of study and verified his results. And how about Mr. Backster? By measuring electric impulses, he proved that plants even reacted to his thoughts, and that they also had memories."

He stroked the petal of my Phalaenopsis with the nail of his index finger.

"The geometry of plants, their mathematical perfection, never ceases to amaze me. Each flower is a wheel of life, its own microcosm. The development of every plant vindicates the philosophy of eternal return.

"We don't actually know," he continued, "what plants really are. We think they are passive, weak, harmless. What a delusion! The earth holds no greater power than the energy of the plant kingdom. Mankind's clumsy dabbling on the earth cannot compare to such creativity."

THE HERETICS

There are people, such as one of the subscribers to *The New Anomalist*, an old crafts teacher, to whom Swedenborg's angels are as concrete, as real, as the cashier at the local grocery store. Another reader claimed to receive messages from the beyond just by closing her eyes and holding a pen over an empty piece of paper. When she opened her eyes, there was a message, always some kind and comforting words, such as, "It is so beautiful here" or "Everything is fine now."

A third reader wasn't as lucky. He wrote that his home was being terrorized by a poltergeist. It would rattle his wok pan in the kitchenette of his rented one-bedroom apartment and would make his cellphone ring even when he had switched it off. During the night, it would roll up his blanket so that he would wake up shivering from cold and fright. It would even turn on the espresso machine he'd just switched off.

He called *The New Anomalist* to get information on how to exorcise an evil or earthbound spirit. I didn't have anything to give him. All I could say was: "Keep calm and try to ignore it."

He was disappointed. "What a pity that there are no competent exorcists in our parish," he said. I never heard from him again, and I don't know whether the disturbance ever stopped.

Most of our subscribers, however, were completely average people, to whom nothing truly extraordinary ever happened. They read our magazine out of casual interest, seeking novelty, or because they were hungry for sensation.

They were all gnawed at by problems that could not be answered satisfactorily by social awareness, science, religion, art, history, culture, or technological development. In that, too, they were like the rest of humanity. But I did meet several true eccentrics and monomaniacs, or at least corresponded with them. I got attached to some of them, and their likenesses, voices, and obsessions even found their way into my dreams.

It wasn't true that our subscribers were just ignorant morons, as the Marquis would sometimes claim when he was in a bad mood. Our readers were by no means a homogeneous group of people, and some of them were highly educated private thinkers. Many of them were only passionate about a specific, narrow subject. Someone who was interested in synchronisms wouldn't necessarily have any interest in lost continents or the aquatic ape hypothesis.

And let's consider their attitudes towards the connection of mind and body, or mortality and immortality. The readers of *The New Anomalist* had as many opinions on these fundamental questions as any random sample of people. There were those who believed in the immortality of the soul and even that it could evolve to higher planes through reincarnation, eventually reaching divinity. Some thought that individual consciousness lived on for only a short time after the body died, merging then with the world spirit. Others were convinced that it's all over when the brain dies.

All of them couldn't be right, but it was hard to disprove anyone's opinion.

For instance, Saulus once said, "Let's assume that you fall to your death from a cliff one hundred yards high. What's your first thought right after? You think, 'Oh, I didn't die after all!'"

"Saulus," I said, "You are a modern-day heretic."

If only I'd asked, Saulus would have given the Marquis an entire lecture on what the soul is. He would have said: First we must examine what the body is.

Saulus believed that there were seven levels of consciousness and humans had seven bodies. Only two of them exist on the physical plane, the physical and etheric bodies. Our third body is the astral body. The body, therefore, consists of a physical side, which we experience through our senses. We can feel its weight, and are forced to give it up at the moment of death. But the body consists of so much more. The astral body is the same as our personal consciousness, whereas the mental body could be called our soul or ego. Seven levels lie between pure spiritual consciousness and physical consciousness, Saulus claimed.

"What?" I once asked Saulus. "You're mixing up bodies and souls. Isn't that a bit strange?"

"It's a mistake to think that these things would be simple," Saulus replied. "You say my words are confusing. But what do you think of the latest scientific theories? Now those are unbelievable, wouldn't you say? They want us to believe that elementary particles can be in two places at the same time. And even that's not enough! Recently I heard a hypotheses that it's likely that the world we perceive actually behaves like the world of atoms—we're just not aware of it."

"What does that mean?"

"It means that the chair that we're sitting on or the apple we're about to sink our teeth into is simultaneously in some other place. What do you say to that? And not just in *some* other place, but in an infinite number of other places, and not just the chair we sit on or the apple we bite into, but first and foremost the person sitting in the chair or eating the apple. You see, some scientists suggest that there are countless universes. They say that every possible state of affairs must have its own universe, and hence these new universes are born all the time. Apparently, this is the logical result of quantum theory."

"Fine, then," I said. "Of course it sounds incredible. But nevertheless, it's a theory that has been created to explain something otherwise unexplainable. In a way, it's incredibility is necessary. Unlike your theory."

"How do you figure that?" Saulus asked, somewhat offended.

"Well, for example, who's to say that there aren't six or eight levels between pure spiritual and raw physical consciousness?"

"Because it's been known for centuries that there are seven," Saulus said.

"Known by whom?" I asked.

"By the holders of secret wisdom," he replied.

OLD FAITH

Whenever the Marquis would run off to the library or the bar or wherever, Faith, his aged dog, would often stay with me the whole day. She's a mutt, half-spaniel, half-collie. She's black and white like a yin and yang.

Once upon a time, she was a weanling, a sleepy and whimpering puppy. Once upon a time she darted after candy wrappers whirling in the wind, learned to sit and shake and heel, barked at squirrels, dug holes in the compost heap, stalked the shadow that the smoke from the coffee roastery cast on the pavement.

Every species has its time. A dog's time seems so short from the human perspective. Ten or twelve years pass, and adult humans are almost the same as before, or at least they think they are. But the course of Faith's life is already nearing nightfall. The fur of her black spots has turned a shade of silver at the ends. Faith is almost deaf. There's no use in calling her name when she's ambling ahead of me. She can't hear my call in the midst of city's clamor.

Faith is on a special low-protein diet to slow the failing of her kidneys. She suffers from a weak heart, and each morning a bitter tablet has to be crushed and mixed into her lean food.

Her dignified and melancholy being, full of a sort of underlying sorrow, gives the room a distinct atmosphere. It becomes filled with her presence.

From where does that melancholy stem? Not just from old age. Every dog has the same problem. Their lives are balancing acts between a humanized being and a older, wilder nature. Dogs are interstitial beings, not yet human, but no longer wolves. That is the unresolved paradox of doghood. There is no returning to the past—or if there is, it would mean a total break of their bond with humans—but humanity is also a mystery to them, something they can never attain.

When Faith looks out the window, I study her profile. The small movements of her eyes reveal what's happening outside. When Faith gets tired, and nowadays that happens from lighter and lighter exertions, she lies down with a grunt on the Chinese doormat, the one decorated with the image of a blue dragon. I see Faith dreaming. Her eyelids and the dark corners of her mouth move, her heavy paws tremble as if she were dreaming of running in a summer meadow.

At times I think how strange and wonderful it is that a completely different species of mammal participates so closely in our lives. I watch these lowly creatures, the ones we call dogs, just dogs. I watch the movements of their ears, the patterns and color schemes of their coats, the various types of tails they have and the expressiveness of these tails, and I am filled with deep awe.

I see these four-legged creatures stroll obediently by their masters or pull frantically at their leashes in a direction of their own choosing. I see them sniffing around and playing in parks, I see them in trains and buses, tied up in front of stores, waiting paitiently for their owners, panting in the heat. No city or town soundscape could be complete without the sound of dogs barking. How much less lively and more impoverished this city would be without the participation of dogs. Much of our thoughts and daily doings fall beyond dogs' understanding. These creatures are not concerned with buying and selling, election-year opinion polls, the downfall of the Nepalese royal family or the Tobin tax. The universe of smells and memories, the sphere in which dogs live, extends beyond our reach. The things that grab our attention, our sense of time, the sensitivity of our senses, and our entire perception are different.

And yet we can make contact with each other, and that, if anything, is a miracle in my opinion.

The spiritual bond between dog and human is different, more durable and resilient, than the bond we have with any other animal. It cannot be severed. It cannot be disowned.

I often talk to Faith. No one listens to me better than she does, tilting her head, taking in my every nuance of tone and state of mind. She understands the jist, I have no doubt about that. Her inquisitive, intense gaze could easily be called human.

But no, why would she be human? Only because she is so full of consciousness?

Faith knows before anyone else when her master is coming to the office. Half an hour before the Marquis arrives, she will lie down by the front door. She won't sleep, only grunt now and then to herself.

When I was a child, I had a German picture book called *Tiere sehen Dich an*. The shining black gaze of an ostrich from the height of its long neck and the round, thoughtful eyes of a monkey dressed in a colorful children's jacket. The convict gaze of a fox being farmed for its fur, trapped behind the chicken wire of its cage.

Victims, friends, colleagues, housemates, pets... Even when we live together, we live in different worlds. They live in the universes of other senses and perceptions, but our gazes and deeds connect our fates. We feed them and feed on them, we hunt them and clothe ourselves in their skins. Our power over them is terrifying.

The gaze of other species defines humanity, gives us our bearings. How could our own language give us this information? Only in the eyes of a stranger can we read who we are and what we are like.

A LESSON

I was looking at the dust on my desk and thought that maybe it was time to do some cleaning, for the sake of my own health if for no other reason, when Ursula, the building janitor, walked in. I was expecting her.

"What are you looking at?" she asked.

"Just dust," I said.

"Do you know what dust is, where it actually comes from? From volcanoes, distant stars, the cloaks of ancient kings…"

"I'll just wipe it off," I said. "Then we can begin the lesson."

Ursula, who had studied yoga meditation for decades, had promised to teach me some mind- centering techniques.

"Western people believe in the subconscious, but don't even know the superconscious exists," she said.

"The key is what people focus their attention on," she said. "To become conscious of consciousness, to perceive the perceiver, that takes real skill.

"Our goal is to reach a state of pure consciousness," she said. "It's a lofty goal, but you have to aim high. You have to control the flow of your consciusness and attention and learn to direct it. You do know that you can't focus attention on many things at the same time, don't you?"

I nodded absent-mindedly. I was thinking about an article that had been sent to us, which I'd have to cut. It dealt with how the phases of the moon affect the luck of Las Vegas gamblers.

"Try to focus your attention on the center of your brain. If you lose focus, hold your breath for a while. That usually helps to refocus on the essential."

I did as I was told, held my breath for a while, but it wasn't all that easy to find the center of my brain. I had to let my breath flow again, and I soon became sleepy, forgetting even Las Vegas.

"Sooner or later you will hear sounds at different pitches. They aren't just the hum of your ears and it's not just your ears that you're hearing them with."

I didn't ask her what the sounds were, as I was trying hard to follow her instructions. But a tram turned somewhere on the other side of the block and the screech extinguished all my potential inner sounds. A toilet was flushed upstairs, and someone whistled outside the window, as if giving a prearranged signal.

"Focus on the highest sound and let it lift you higher and higher. Don't listen to it with your left ear, use your right. Move it to the center of your head, where the Sahasrara chakra lies."

"What chakra?" I asked.

"That's not important now. The more you concentrate, the better you can hear that sound. When you learn to follow it, it'll fill your body, your whole environment, and some day, when you open your eyes afterwards, everything around you will be blindingly bright, even at midnight."

I remembered the nocturnal lights that I'd seen with my eyes closed and not open. I wondered whether I had unwittingly practiced the method Ursula was now teaching me. But the sound that she was talking about, that I didn't remember having heard. Only a whistle.

"If this technique doesn't work, close your eyes and focus on the spot that is between your eyebrows, the place that's called the center of the third eye. Can you see different colored figures floating in the dark?"

As I watched them, I happened to remember an interview with a woman, who had recently lost her sight. "People think that the blind see only darkness," she'd said. "That's not true. I'm never in the darkness. Shapes of various colors swim in front of me in a mist. I try not to pay any attention to them."

With my eyes closed, I kept thinking about blindness and how, if you were blind from birth, you wouldn't be able to know that you were missing something unless you knew someone who could see.

"Are you listening to me?" Ursula asked.

"Sorry."

"Can you see figures?"

"Yes, pale rings or loops."

"Follow their movement and transformation as if you were watching a film. Focus on the smallest one and push through it."

I tried to do that, but the figure expanded into a cloud of mist and I opened my eyes. I didn't feel like I'd gotten much out of the lesson, and I think Ursula sensed my disappointment.

"It's a process that takes a lot of time and determination," she said. "It couldn't really be any other way. Pure consciousness is divinity. If you're patient, if you learn real focus, you'll get closer to it. Did you know that chakras are like flowers, like flower petals of spiraling light?"

When she said that, I thought about the datura. There was something sacred about that plant.

After Ursula had gone, I vacuumed and emptied the trash can.

"It sure is clean in here today," said the Marquis, who came in just as I had organized the papers on my desk into three comparatively neat stacks. I hadn't heard his usual knock. He looked around with approval.

I looked around as well. I was fairly content with what I saw. The office actually looked cozy.

"There were too many cloaks of ancient kings in here," I said.

He didn't ask what on earth I was talking about.

"I see you've fought against disorder and entropy. That is the right path, the purpose of mankind on this earth."

I looked at the Marquis, surprised. He didn't ordinarily talk in such a pompous and preacherly manner.

"But have you ever thought that chaos might be the sum of order, that sensible details could build a senseless whole, and not the other way around, as we'd so much like to believe. Quite a terrible thought, isn't it? Think about it," he said and left again before I had time to say anything.

But I agreed that it was a terrible thought.

Half an hour later there was a knock on the door, the Marquis returned, and said again, "It sure is clean in here today. Have you finished the article on the Voynich manuscript?"

"Not yet," I said. "First I have to cut down that Las Vegas article. But what was it that you were talking about earlier?"

"I'm sorry, when?"

"Half an hour ago. You said something about the fundamental senselessness of the universe…"

"This is my first visit here today," the Marquis said and looked at me slowly. "You're not making any sense yourself. Maybe you should take some time off."

My heart ran cold. He was lying to me. I couldn't believe it. I didn't want to consider the obvious and even more repellent alternative: that he was telling the truth.

NICOLA'S FORMATIVE YEARS

Nicola Tesla has been dubbed the man who invented the twentieth century. And yet this scholar and inventor, the father of the radio, alternating current, wireless communication, the induction motor, and many others, was forgotten for decades. Now those who chase after free energy and believe in perpetual motion machines swear by Tesla's name, and online you can order Tesla mosquito repellent, Tesla biomagnets, and Tesla space oil.

Nicola Tesla was born in Smiljan, Croatia, in 1856. Already as a child he was clearly an extraordinary individual of unusual skill. A powerful imagination and awe-inspiring memory, clarity and purity of thought defined his life from his early years on. His orthodox father wanted Nicola to become a priest, while Nicola himself set his sights on becoming an engineer.

He was hypersensitive to smells and other sensory stimuli. A piece of camphor somewhere in the house gave him fits of extreme disgust. If Asperger's syndrome had been known in his time, he probably would have been diagnosed with it.

"I would not touch the hair of other people except, perhaps, at the point of a revolver," he once wrote.

Tesla could certainly be said to have had hyperhearing. Nicola saved his neighbours from fires several times, as his hearing was so sensitive that he could not only hear the ticking of a clock several rooms away, but also the small crackles made by a fire igniting miles away.

According to his own claims, Nicola could also levitate. In his short autobiography he wrote:

> "Like most children I was fond of jumping and developed
> an intense desire to support myself in the air. Occasionally
> a strong wind richly charged with oxygen blew from the
> mountains rendering my body as light as cork and then I
> would leap and float in space for a long time."

Already at an early age, Nicola's mother led him in memory exercises,
the quality of which Tesla doesn't specify. He later continued mental
exercises, demonstrating admirable self-discipline. The catalyst for
these exercises was a novel by the Hungarian author Jósika. According
to Nicola, it awakened his willpower.

"After years of such discipline I gained so complete a mastery over
myself that I toyed with passions which have meant destruction to
some of the strongest men," he—otherwise such a modest person—
boasts.

Tesla does not specify the nature of the passions he refers to. His
autobiography does mention gambling, to which he was addicted
in his youth for a time. On sexual matters, Tesla is silent. As far as
is known, he never had relationships with women, nor did he have
homosexual ones. His whole being and life was marked by a sort of
innocense and puritanism, also extending to his financial matters.

After seeing an avalanche form from a small snowball, he wondered
at how great events can grow out of small deeds. This awe inspired by
the laws of nature stayed with him to the end of his days.

Nicola had an exceptionally developed ability of visualization.
From early on, he could see with his mind's eye all the details of entire
systems with motors and generators that didn't yet exist. He saw them
functioning, he could make out their material, the shining and hard
metal. The images or films were as real as any object before his eyes.

These visions soon began to flow in front of his eyes in an endless
stream. In less than two months he invented several new types and
variations of motor.

Tesla writes of having once strolled down a riverbank with his uncle.
The sun was setting and trout seemed to be playing as they were

hunting. Now and then one of them would leap into the air, and its shimmering body would stand out against the rock face on the other side of the river.

Nicola told his uncle what he intended to do. He would hurl a stone at a trout, so that it would slam against the rock and be cut in two. He picked up a stone and in the next moment did exactly what he'd promised. His uncle was so thoroughly frightened that he yelled: "*Vade retro, Satanas!*"

Days went by before he spoke to his nephew again.

When studying at the higher Real Gymnasium in Carlstadt, Croatia, Nicola lived with his aunt, who fed him like a canary. The meals were refined and delicious, but very frugal. Tesla writes that he suffered like Tantalus, but turned this, too, to his advantage.

At the Polytechnic School in Gratz, Tesla completed an unbelievable number of degrees in a short time. His professors wrote to his father and asked him to take his son out of the school, so that he wouldn't kill himself from overexhaustion.

In Budapest, Nicola suffered a severe nervous breakdown. His senses were sensitized to the point of it being an illness. A fly walking on the table was like a hollow hammering in his head. He had a hard time walking under bridges, because he felt their crushing weight in his skull. The whistle of a locomotive engine thirty miles away made the chair underneath him tremble so that the pain was almost unbearable.

Nicola felt that the ground beneath him was constantly shaking. (This reminds me of Strindberg, who complained while living in Paris that the city was continuously trembling.)

His eyesight also became so acute that he could make his way in the darkness like a bat and could distinguish objects at a distance before anyone else noticed the first sign of them.

Tesla's pulse fluctuated strongly and could rise up to 260. He was pestered by muscle spasms. He could recite complete novels from memory. One day Tesla was reciting *Faust* to his friend, verses that described the evening sun: "*Sie rückt und weicht, der Tag ist überlebt, Dort eilt sie hin und fordert neues Leben...*" He then describes having had a flare in his brain like a lightning bolt, a new vision. He drew a diagram of the induction motor in the sand.

"I cannot begin to describe my emotions. Pygmalion seeing his statue come to life could not have been more deeply moved," Tesla wrote.

The Second Seed Pod

The Pendulum Man and Un-Me

Before eating anything, even at a restaurant, The Pendulum Man would always use his pendulum, a four-inch-long piece of string weighted with a five mark coin on the end. He claimed that this instrument told him whether the food was edible and if it was suitable for his digestion.

"I have a very sensitive stomach," he said. "It starts growling very easily."

And, indeed, at that very moment, I thought I heard a sound like an irritated dog growling somewhere out of sight.

The Pendulum Man had written us a short article about his experiences of being a pendulum man. He said that I could treat him to a good lunch, as he wouldn't accept payment for his article.

I took him to an Italian restaurant, where he ordered just soup. I watched him dangle the pendulum above his minestrone. The coin swung lazily back and forth, back and forth. I watched both amused and nervous. He had explained to me that if the pendulum started making circles, he would unfortunately have to decline eating the food. But the coin didn't change its path, and I gave a sigh of relief when he finally picked up his spoon.

"Hang on a minute," he said, his spoon halting mid-way. "Should we see what it has to say about your food?"

I'd already started to eat my tortellinis, which tasted delicious, and

I didn't want to risk having the pendulum steal my meal from me, so I politely declined.

"The pendulum knows. Although to the question of whether the food is edible, it can only answer yes or no," he said. "But that's all it has to do."

Only after we'd emptied our plates did I let him teach me the basics of pendulum use.

"The pendulum should hang freely, held between the thumb and forefinger. It will start swinging lightly back and forth. That's oscillation," he said.

"I see," I said and tried to keep my hand steady.

"Sooner or later the movement becomes circular. When that happens depends on the element in question. The pendulum has a different reaction to different materials, even colors," he said. "The number of revolutions the pendulum makes varies. Iron, copper, silver, they all have their own trajectories."

He said many other things as well, told me his pendulum's exact trajectories for several different materials, but now I can remember only silver: 56 centimeters and 22 revolutions.

"By the way, if I put a strip of aluminum foil on my forehead, the pendulum no longer answers my questions correctly," the Pendulum Man told me.

"But doesn't that just go to show that it's all about some human ability and not the pendulum itself? Have you considered that the movements of your hands unconsciously control the pendulum?" I asked him.

"Of course," he said. "That's exactly what I think. Unconsciously, that's the important word! In fact, the pendulum works better when I don't focus on it particularly. You see, it's not me controlling the pendulum. It is un-me."

"*Un*-me?" I asked.

"Precisely. You see, the pendulum also reacts to completely abstract things, such as thoughts and emotions. In fact, the pendulum reacts only to those, as material objects are just forms of thought to it. It communicates with our consciousness, or more precisely our unconscious. That is the un-me, a tremendous being, several beings you could say, that know so much more than the conscious mind. The un-me gathers information with incredible efficiency. It then mediates those vast amounts of information to our consciousness through the pendulum. Without the un-me we couldn't survive in this world.

"The pendulum has its foibles," the Pendulum Man said at the end of his demonstration. "Can you imagine that a small drop of whiskey substantially improves its precision? I wonder why that is? I don't know why, but I've noticed that four centiliters—no more, no less—is the ideal dosage for the pendulum."

I took the hint and ordered the ideal dosage of scotch along with coffee and mille-feuille. The Pendulum Man downed the whiskey to the health of his instrument, and lo and behold! The coin at the end of the string did seem to revolve at a more lively pace above the mille-feuille.

THE PUDDLE

"Take a look at this," I said to Penjami. I passed him a small, black plastic box. "You can have it."

"What is it?"

He took the box carefully in his hands and shook it.

"It rattles."

"Open it," I said.

He peeked inside the box.

"Are those bones?"

"They're supposed to be," I said. "Of course, they're not real. They're fake bones. Tip them out onto the table and turn off the light."

"Why?"

"You'll see."

He stretched out his hand and turned off the lamp with the green lamp shade. The white bones, thin as matches, glowed on the table and illuminated his young face.

"Wow," he said, enchanted, "they're glow-in-the-dark."

"Yes, it's a glow-in-the-dark skeleton puzzle. You can put it together now if you like. You can test it. Your father bought thirty of them, for the parastore. I want to make sure that they really make a complete skeleton. Otherwise the customers will complain and we'll have to give them their money back."

"This was a very small person," he said, contemplative. "A very small toy person," he corrected himself.

I remember well the first time I met little Penjami. It was October, after weeks of rain.

"This here is Penjami," the Marquis said.

Penjami had on blue overalls and a red bomber's hat. He was about four feet tall then. He didn't pay me much attention. He stood in front of the largest puddle in the yard and looked at it with deep, thoughtful eyes.

The old factory building in which *The New Anomalist* was published is located at the lowest point of the street, and its front yard tends to stay moist even in dry weather. The pavement is uneven, the asphalt cracked. Especially after rain, the yard is covered by a network of slowly drying puddles, to the nuisance of bypassers.

"Hi!" I said.

"Hi," Penjami replied absent-mindedly, still not looking at me. "I wonder where you got that puddle?"

"Hm," I said. It was a novel and unexpected question. I had to think for a minute before answering.

"Where was it again… I think we bought it from that grocery store on the corner," I said.

He lifted his grave gaze from the puddle and seemed to see me for the first time. He wasn't the slightest bit amused by my answer.

"Oh."

"I think it was on sale," I said.

"Was it? How much did it cost?" he asked. "Do they still have them?"

"Do you want one like that? Are you sure it's the right size? Not too big or too small?"

He nodded. "It's neat."

I looked at the puddle and saw that he was right. It really was a neat puddle, although I'd never been able to look at it that way before. A miraculous looking-glass, fallen from a cloud. The puddle itself lay in the shadow of the factory, but the cloudless autumn day that it partially reflected made it look deep and pure. The bird that flew across the sky also swam in our puddle. There was a small heaven in our yard. I was thankful to Penjami for making me understand the value of the puddle, and I felt embarrassed that I had teased him.

"Actually you can only get puddles from the sky, not the store. You just have to wait for it to rain," I said. "And then, of course, there has to be a suitable place for a puddle."

"Yeah," he said and fell silent. Now his eyes examined the old factory warehouse critically. "Did you build this?" he asked.

"No, not me," I said. "I just work here. This is an old factory, older than me. Can you believe that?"

"The person who built this building was really smart," he continued.

"What makes you think that?" I asked.

"Because he built it in just the right place."

"How so?" I asked.

"This close to the puddle," little Penjami said.

A Visit to the Hair Artiste

Sometimes the Marquis decided that my duties as subeditor included making house calls. Most of the time it was a task I was reluctant to do, and I tried to explain to the chief editor that it wasn't customary at publishing houses to have their subeditors running around visiting the homes of their readers and contributors.

"But it is our custom," the Marquis simply said.

It was extremely awkward to have to enter the territory of a stranger, step into the circle of their smells and memories. Every time I came back from these house calls, my asthma was worse and a headache would start to throb in my left temple.

"Häikälä the Hair Artiste called today," the Marquis said. "She has some interesting documents, photos apparently, and she insisted that someone come over and take a look at them."

"I see," I said and tried in vain to concentrate on my article on the Voynich manuscript. I knew what was coming and who that someone would be.

"Maybe you could pay her a visit…"

"I'm sure she can just send her photos to us," I said. "Or come over herself."

"No, she's afraid they'll get lost in the mail."

"So what? We certainly don't have to dance to the tune of her fears."

"I already promised her," the Marquis said.

I let out a sigh of submission. "Is a hair artiste the same as a hair dresser?" I asked aloud.

"I guess it's a more respected title," the Marquis replied.

On my way to visit the Hair Artiste, I drove by a building that summoned up an unpleasant memory. I'd never been inside, nor did the building itself have any repellent qualities as such. On the contrary, it was well-proportioned for a building its size, neat and recently painted a pale shade of yellow. But in my early youth it had served as a slaughterhouse.

I took a bus to school that, towards the end of its route along the highway, passed by this building I didn't like to think about what was happening inside the building. I saw those actions as a crime that we all tolerated and had gotten used to, or even worse: a crime we all wished for, without which we couldn't dream of living.

A scene is etched into my mind. It caught my eye years ago while I stood, hemmed in by winter coats, in the aisle at the front of that bus. It was strange, nearly incomprehensible, and I have wondered whether I truly saw it or only imagined the whole thing.

Right before descending to the street below, the highway ran for some twenty yards at the level of the third floor of the building. That day I looked straight into the building through a window and saw a room or a hallway. The only furniture I could make out was a long and narrow table.

On the table lay a woman in a white flower-patterned summer dress, the kind of pattern that was popular at the time. She was maybe the same age as my mother. She lay on her back, motionless, her dark hair spread around her head. I'm no longer certain whether there were other people around her, but I was left with that impression.

The bus drove on. A reddish-white cloud drifted up from the chimney of the coffee- roasting factory. A terrible thought had burned into my mind, an impossible and sickening one.

The memory of that thought was still with me as I parked in the asphalt yard of the Hair Artiste's white brick duplex. The house had Spanish style arches and a hipped roof. The windows had draped curtain arrangements, and the window sills were covered with hand-painted porcelain cats

To my horror , the Hair Artiste, a lady nearing retirement who had blue highlights in her silvery hair, wanted to give me a grand tour of her home, which I politely tried to decline. I told her that *The Anomalist* was not an interior design magazine. With a noticeable air of satisfaction, she walked ahead of me from room to room: the kitchen with French oak cupboards and new copper pots and pans on open shelves; the living room with a sofa upholstered in shiny lurex; the bedroom with a bed spread that the Hair Artiste had designed herself and that had dried rose petals sewn into it.

All through the house, mirrors of various sizes reflected my long nose back at me, and many times I bumped accidentally into unstable little faux rococo tables covered with candelabras, more porcelain animals, dried flower arrangements, ornate mantel clocks, and gilded picture frames. They held not only photos of her relatives, but also of her well-groomed celebrity customers.

"This is my office," she said, and opened yet another door.

I expected the room to have yet more mirrors and a hairdresser's chair and that it would be the place where she received customers who wanted the services of a hair artiste instead of just a regular hairdresser. There was a mirror, a tall trumeau mirror, but instead of a hairdresser's chair there was an ordinary office chair and a writing desk, on which stood a tall pile of hair styling magazines.

"This is where I work on my doctoral thesis," the Hair Artiste said. "I'm in a Ph.D. program."

I must have looked astonished as the Hair Artiste explained that even cosmetologists, hair artistes, and confectioners had Ph.D. programs.

"The topic of my thesis is 'Hairstyles at the Presidential Independence Day Ball across the Decades,' " she told me. "But let's go to my son's room. There is a photograph there that will surely interest you."

Without knocking, she opened the door to a room that gave the impression of having been staged to look like it belonged to a typical schoolboy. Airplanes on the wallpaper and model aircraft hanging from the ceiling. I was bewildered by the computer that I saw on the writing desk. It was a model so ancient that it belonged in a museum. The room was very tidy, so much so that it didn't actually seem lived in.

"Is your son at school?" I asked. I was a bit surprised that a woman her age could have children that were still in school.

"Not in school, not even in the school of life," she replied. "Up there," she pointed toward the ceiling.

I got to listen as she explained that her only son had died of meningitis at the age of fourteen. She had preserved the room untouched for the last ten years.

"This is where I keep my photo albums," she said. "Just a few days ago I noticed something odd. Hold on."

She opened the top drawer of the writing desk and took out an album.

"Come sit here next to me," she said, and patted the steering wheel pattern blanket on her son's narrow bed.

I sat and waited gloomily as she leafed through her album. I didn't want to stay in that room, or in that house, any longer than I had to.

"Here it is! Take a look! It was taken right here. The last photo of my son."

The colors of the photograph had faded. A young boy with blond hair sat at the desk, maybe in the middle of building a model aircraft. He looked completely engrossed in what he was doing and wasn't looking at the camera.

"Either this picture has changed," the Hair Artiste said, "or I just haven't noticed it before."

"Changed in what way?" I asked.

"A new shadow has appeared in the photo, right here," the Hair Artiste said, and pointed at the wall behind the boy in the photograph. "Do you see it?"

I looked. Indeed, a broad shadow could be seen on the airplane wallpaper. What was there to say about it? Was this really the reason I'd been sent out on a house call?

"Can't you see?"

I saw the shadow, but what was she expecting me to say?

"It's the shadow of a wing! Can you see the ends of the feathers? See, it starts right by my son's shoulder. And there isn't anything in the room that could cast a shadow like that. I took the picture, so I know for sure. And you know what else? This picture was taken just three days before he died. That very night he fell ill, and he fell into a coma the next day in the hospital."

I looked at the dark shadow of a wing on the wall, and the pain in the woman's voice tore at my heart.

"Now he has his wings," the mother said. "I know he's earned them."

"Such a beautiful picture," I said. "And such a beautiful boy. This is a precious memory of him. But…"

And I had to tell her, as delicately as possible, that that beauty and the miracle in the photo were of no use to *The New Anomalist*.

"I wish you all the best with your doctoral thesis," I said as I was leaving.

"If you ever need your hair done for a party, call me," she said.

She'd already forgiven me for not wanting to publish the picture of her son, who had become an angel.

"There's nothing I couldn't do with hair like yours."

DON'T BE CRUEL

The parastore had gotten new wares. A rock 'n' roll fish, for example.
I'd tried everything to prevent the Marquis from adding it to our
selection, but in vain. We now had one hundred sixty fish in stock.
They were everywhere: in the bathroom and under the desk and piled
on top of the hat rack. I was sure that the fish was a bad investment,
but the Marquis insisted that it was super popular in many countries
and that it had sold in the hundreds of thousands.

I hated that atrocity. You couldn't even make out what species of
fish it was. It was made out of plastic or fiberglass and activated by a
motion sensor. When an unsuspecting person came within a foot of
it, it would start to sing and shake its tail.

The packaging said: Natural design! High quality! Enjoy you friends'
amazed faces when the fish surprises them with its song and dance!

"What kind of fish is it even supposed to be?" I asked the Marquis.

"Hmm. It could be a pikeperch, or maybe an arctic char? What
difference does it make?" the Marquis said. "Or it could be some
American fish. I don't think I've seen anything like it in this corner of
the world."

"I have to know what species it is in case a potential customer
shows up and asks me, though I have to admit that I have a hard time
believing anyone would want to waste their money on something like
this."

"The world is full of imbeciles," the Marquis said. "They're never
in short supply. I've pinned my hopes to them. I admit it's hard to

imagine anyone wanting to waste their money on this. Did I mention that hundreds of thousands of these have been sold worldwide?"

"You did. But what does this monster have to do with the paranormal and *The Anomalist*?"

"Wouldn't you call a fish that sings and dances an anomaly? Listen to this!" The Marquis pushed a button.

The abomination lifted its head. Its tail began to flap. It opened its jaws, and I peeked in. I saw a salmon-red cavity filled with white plastic spikes and a small speaker that was blaring, "Don't be cruel!" Apparently the fish was a contra tenor.

The Marquis tilted his head to listen, pleased with both the fish and himself.

"Turn it off, please," I said. "Judging by its voice at least, it's a sleazy kind of fish. Does it know any other tunes?"

"It should also sing 'All Shook Up,' " the Marquis said. "Should we give it a listen?"

"No, never mind. I have work to do."

"Look, it even has a wonderful little stand so that you can put it on your desk."

"For God's sake, don't put that nightmare on my desk!"

"On the bookshelf then."

"Does this mean that every time I go to the bookshelf to get something, it's going to start singing 'Don't be Cruel'?"

"Or 'All Shook Up.' But there must be an off-button somewhere," the Marquis said.

"Find it," I said.

The rock 'n' roll fish made me so very depressed. I started to think about how that kind of junk was manufactured, and it made me want to cry. I thought that maybe there was a person out there somewhere, a single mother perhaps, who had to get up at 5:50 a.m. every morning to go to work at the rock 'n' roll fish factory.

She drinks a cup of cheap instant coffee and then wakes up her anemic little child. Feeds and dresses it and puts it in a pram. Waits for the bus in the rain to take her crying, fatherless offspring to the daycare center across town. Then she takes the rush-hour metro, bus, or maybe both, to the industrial area on the northern fringe of the city. She punches in and, under the cruel glow of the fluorescent lights in the prefabricated factory hall, assembles an endless procession of fish. Shoves batteries and speakers into their guts and glues plastic fins to their backs or stands to their bellies. She does this from seven till noon, eats leftover tuna casserole for lunch, and goes on and on.

The winter sun has already set, but still I see her thin hunched neck in front of me. Her legs are aching by now. Her armpits are sweaty, her ankles cold. I can see her pale, unfailing fingers as she tests the fish. Each one activates in turn and sings to her, "Don't be cruel!" "I'm all shook up!"

The Face in the Cheese

The seed pod of the datura plant is the size of a walnut and is covered in small thorns. When it ripens and splits open, four compartments with light brown, asymmetrical inhabitants are revealed.

That day was the most bitterly cold we'd had that winter. I had just opened one seed pod and shaken out its contents into a small ceramic cup when the phone rang.

"We have, in our kitchen, just witnessed a miracle," a breathless woman's voice said.

"What kind of a miracle?" I asked cautiously.

The lady on the other end of the line was calling from the north. She'd bought a piece of bread cheese from the local dairy, twenty-one ounces, she explained to me. A national delicacy, bread cheese is flat, tasteless, and slightly rubbery. The rounds are baked, which gives the cheese its distinctive brown spots. Nevertheless, many people find it delicious, especially when served with jam.

The woman and her husband had planned to enjoy some freshly baked bread cheese with their afternoon coffee, but before they could get that far, the wife noticed a certain recognizable image in a cluster of dark spots.

"You'll never believe what it is." she said, lowering her voice to indicate confidentiality. I waited.

"A face," she said. "The face of our Lord."

I didn't know how to react. Finally, I managed to say, "Really. To think. That's quite…"

"You can even see His crown of thorns. Our neighbors came by to look at the cheese and they also recognized Him right away," the lady said. "I never thought I'd be blessed in this way! We thought we'd offer your magazine an opportunity. You can come and take a photo of it, exclusively. The whole piece of cheese is still in the fridge. We haven't touched it, and we don't plan to."

I thanked her for the offer and said that the case was interesting as such and quite unusual, but unfortunately we were very busy at the moment and didn't have anyone available to take such a long trip.

"Who was it?" the Marquis asked me, once I had hung up after brief good-byes. I hadn't seen the man in over a week, but now he'd just happened to stop by to pick up some correspondence related to pyramidology.

I told him a miracle had happened. Not exactly the apparition of the Virgin Mary, but something similar. Jesus had appeared in bread cheese.

"Hmm. That would make a good 'Picture of the Week,' " the Marquis said.

"You can't be serious," I said.

"That's actually a brilliant idea. Why don't you do a human interest piece. Take your camera and drive up there first thing in the morning."

"That's two hundred-fifty miles! For a piece of cheese? Is that your idea of human interest?"

"It is," the Marquis said coldly. "You can spend the night at a motel."

The temperature rose quickly the next day, though it stayed below freezing. I informed the bread cheese woman that *The New Anomalist* was interested in her apparition after all. She was delighted. I drove two hundred-fifty miles in a blizzard, the last fifty miles crawling along narrow village roads behind a snowplow, passing an art barn, a sheep-farm-cum-craft-shop, and a village grocery shop that had been converted into an interactive café.

Now and then, I had the unpleasant feeling that someone was sitting in the back seat. It was a new phenomenon, a hollow twinge of fear, that I hadn't experienced prior to that winter. A few times I even glanced behind me and almost lost control of the car on the slippery road.

The house was a typical small wooden house of the kind built by veterans after World War II, pale green, one-and-a-half floors high. A flower pot had been hung on the porch next to the door. The heather inside it had frozen. Snow had piled up over three jalopies parked behind the sauna cottage in the yard. The man of the house probably spent his retirement fixing them.

The woman I had spoken to on the phone came to greet me. She sat me down on a couch amid embroidered cushions. Behind the couch was a woven wall hanging, which I thought depicted Leda and the Swan, though the bird in it looked more like a goose.

"Why don't we have some coffee first and then you can see Him," she said. "You do have your camera with you? You'll be amazed, I promise. It's just like an icon."

Only more ephemeral, I thought to myself.

I drank a cup of coffee accompanied by homemade sugar cookies. Heartburn was rising in my gullet by the time the apparition was brought in, and I couldn't hold back a burp. The cheese had been placed in a crystal bowl, maybe even a christening bowl, which in turn had been placed on a doily. I can't say that I was impressed.

"There!" the lady said victoriously, and pointed with her finger. The guidance was very necessary. A sympathetic eye could just make out a splotch resembling a human face in the pattern of spots on the surface of the cheese, just like you can see human faces, hats, churches, and cats, in stained wallpaper, fluffy clouds, or the wood fibers of a table.

"Oh," I said. I wasn't able to manage much more enthusiasm, though I realized that the woman was disappointed by my lame reaction. This house call was starting to remind of me the visit to the Hair Artiste. I decided to give the Marquis a few choice words when I got back to the city.

"Just think," the woman said, "I don't believe this cheese will ever get moldy. It's still as if it's freshly baked, don't you think?"

I didn't think that at all, but held my tongue. To me, the cheese already smelled somewhat suspicious. Upon closer inspection, its dried-up edges already had a tinge of green to them.

I drank my coffee and took some photos of the cheese, as the Marquis had insisted. I'd never had a more ridiculous assignment. I asked the woman a couple of questions, so that I could say that I'd interviewed her. "Where did you buy the cheese? Did you notice the face right away? Has anything like this happened to you before?"

I soon ran out of questions. I felt hopeless, and everything around me looked ugly and banal. The cushions, Leda, and, above all, the miracle of the cheese.

Her answers also became short and bland. I realized that the woman was disappointed in her interview and that both of us were eagerly waiting for the visit to end.

"The bible circle from Sorainen parish is coming tomorrow. A whole bus load," she told me on the porch, as I was taking my leave.

"To come look at the cheese?"

"The cheese, of course," the woman said. "And on Wednesday another bus load is coming from Kätkälä. I'm charging them a small fee, compensation for the extra cleaning. They track in so much mud on their shoes."

I looked down, concerned, but I'd taken my shoes off as soon as I had entered. But the woman still seemed to have something on her chest.

"I gave you exclusive rights to the story," she said. "So…"

"Do you mean—?"

"Well, I think some sort of small reward would be in order," she said. "This being a miracle and all. I did give you exclusive rights."

"We don't usually…We didn't discuss anything like this."

The air between us grew even colder.

"On the other hand," I said to get myself out of the situation, "maybe we could give you all this year's issues free of charge?"

"I don't know," she said. "It being a miracle and all."

"And next year's as well," I said in a panic.

"Well, alright then," she consented, still clearly dissatisfied.

I felt relieved once I'd closed the door behind me, and my mood improved quickly. The blizzard had eased up, the temperature had dropped again, and the starlit sky shone above me. From the cold earth, I looked up into even an greater coldness. I looked at the misty belt of the galaxy, and in the emptiness made out the constellations that human eyes had invented and named.

In the few steps that I took beneath Ursa Major from the porch to the car, I had time to think: Why did I think the woman was strange and look down on her for seeing the face of her Savior in a piece of cheese? What about the faces in the flowers, the stars, and the symbols in the Voynich manuscript? Or the Hair Artiste and the shadow of a wing in her photograph? And didn't Mr. Chance, too, see a deeper meaning in coincidence?

Every eye roams the indifference of the universe in search of signs, figures, images, messages. They can be found everywhere in the cosmos once you learn to see with human sight. Who's to say whether it's a strength or a weakness? It's the way human beings are made, the way we're born. Why is it that life and meaning seem to spring up wherever we humans direct our attention?

The car wouldn't start at first, but once the engine warmed up and I got onto the dark road, I felt that my head was clearer than it had been for a long time, and now no one was sitting in the back seat.

Would it show more courage to acknowledge right away that humans don't have a special place in the universe and that our fate is no more important than that of individual cell? We lonely souls playing with our strange brains under this brief sun should not be called cowards.

The road led home and south.

LOOGAROO, A CLASSIC

Her name is Loogaroo. A beautiful name, like a song or a distant mating call. Loogaroo herself is beautiful as well, in an unapproachable, exotic way. Her hair falls on her shoulders in a shining bronze swirl, her satin shirt is an iridescent black, and her pale skin, either powdered white or just naturally that unusual shade, glimmers like moonlit snow. Her nose is pierced, with a silver ball hanging from it. She wears a dog's collar, the kind with metal spikes. She, if anyone, is "cool."

I realize that here before me is a woman who could drive men mad, who could make them commit senseless deeds. Despite the fact that she is enchanting in her own way—or maybe because of it—I feel a hint of antipathy toward her. I try to hide it, of course, even though I don't exactly smile at her. The things she says to me put me off.

And she, too, remains stern faced. Throughout the interview, she is grave, solemn, didactic. She's a little over twenty, twenty-five at most. Her attitude could be considered amusing in someone so young if one failed to realize that she is actually a professional of sorts.

Loogaroo senses my dislike, no doubt, and returns the sentiment. She looks down on me. I can see myself from her perspective. I'm an insignificant reporter, a fastidious and conventional everyday person, who sleeps at night and wakes up in the morning well before the eight o'clock news. I am one of the plain cogs of the society she despises.

"Why Loogaroo?" I ask. The recorder in front of me is rolling and humming.

When she speaks, something shiny flashes in her mouth. Her

tongue, too, is pierced. She says she was named after an ancient legend. Long ago in the Caribbean, there lived a woman called Loogaroo. This woman would shed her skin at night and turn into a flame and search for blood to drink.

"But Loogaroo had a strange habit, a sort of compulsion, which would halt her in the middle of her hunt."

"Yes?" I ask, when Loogaroo falls silent.

"If she happened upon a pile of sand, she would stop and count the grains. People who were afraid of being attacked by Loogaroo at night could leave a pile of rice or sand in front of their door in the hope that Loogaroo would stop to count the grains and forget her thirst."

"Do you count grains of sand?" I ask.

"Don't we all?" she asks in turn. "Recount our own deeds?"

The answer takes me by surprise. She looks sad and a bit more human than before.

"How often do you consume human blood?" I ask somewhat harshly, perhaps to hide my surprise.

I feel embarrassed when she responds, "Do you really expect me to answer such an intimate question?"

"You agreed to this interview, and our readers no doubt expect exactly these kinds of questions," I defended myself. "In an interview with a real vampire—which is what you claim to be—I think the question is valid. If you prefer, we can proceed on a general level."

"I'd prefer that."

"Alright, how often do vampires consume blood?"

"There's no exact rule," she replies. "Some fast for up to six months, but there are also those that need a weekly dose. But all of us must consume blood from time to time. Otherwise we die."

"In what other ways do vampires differ from humans?"

"In many ways. I'm sure you know that individuals like me hate sunlight and have excellent night vision."

"I've heard that," I admit.

"Our optic nerves can process low levels of light more efficiently, and therefore we're able to see better in the dark than humans," Loogaroo explains. "Too much light, on the other hand, causes an overload of information, headaches, and visual impairment. Many of us also easily get sunstroke, sun rashes, and heatstroke. In general we are more energetic by night than by day, unlike humans."

I notice that this is the second time that she's said "humans" instead of "other people."

"Do I have this right—that you don't consider yourselves human?" I ask cautiously.

"I don't," she answers firmly. "We are of another race. Our hearing is better, as are our reactions. We're faster, stronger, and healthier than humans. We recover from injuries and illnesses faster than humans. We live substantially longer."

She doesn't look at all healthy to me, anemic and a bit lethargic really, but maybe that's because the sun hasn't set yet. She's just woken up. And maybe she hasn't had her dose of energy drink in a long while? The thought makes me uneasy.

"I am a Classic," she says.

"And what does that mean?" I ask her. "I'm not very deeply acquainted with vampyrology."

"It means that I've become a vampire through infection. I'm not a Natural Born. A retrovirus infection is required to turn a human into a vampire. That can be a long process. but sooner or later, the person's chemistry changes irreversibly."

A retrovirus infection! Though the recorder is running, I write this down in my notebook and feel very old and worn out. Dear God, the things one must do for a living!

The sun sets and I get tired, but Loogaroo seems livelier and more excited. Her lethargy seems to have passed, her eyes glimmering black and gold. She even smiles, shaking her thick, silky mane from time to time.

"You do understand," she says, "that the need for blood is biological, not just psychological. You must also remember that true vampires are always unpredictable. We are potential killers. When our energy levels drop, when the hunger for blood becomes unbearable, we can't help but satisfy our needs."

"Even if it would lead to irreparable consequences?" I ask.

"Even then," she says. "Those kinds of consequences can't always be avoided."

"Should I be on my guard now," I ask her and give a somewhat forced laugh.

She doesn't react to my remark at all, just fixes me with the same superior and distant gaze, as black and pale as before.

After a long pause she remarks, "Haven't you considered that humans also drink and eat each other? They all draw vitality, memories, thoughts, love, and hate from each other? It cannot be helped."

Again she takes me by surprise. A minute passes before I'm able to get back to my questions.

"When you said that you live longer than humans on average, how long do you expect yourself to live? Over a hundred years?"

"Accidents can happen, of course," she answers. "Vampires, too, can be run over by a car. We can be killed, even if it isn't all that easy. But in any case, at least a hundred years."

"And how old are you now?"

"Seventy-three years old," she says. "Seventy-four next month."

She looks completely sincere, the devil. I don't even laugh, I only raise my eyebrows. She really does take me for an idiot.

"Well, I think this is enough," I say and turn off the recorder. "I'll send you the interview to review."

"That won't be necessary," she says.

I realize that she's completely uninterested in whatever I'm going to write. She has already turned her attention to the coming night.

In the Wrong Line

Today I passed a line that stretched around the block. It was taciturn and orderly. No one tried to cut, they all waited patiently for their turn. What were they waiting in line for? Everyone knows, but no one likes to talk about it.

The line shouldn't even exist, but it forms there every day nonetheless. It's partially the same line as yesterday, partially it's new. It seems to grow a little bit longer every day. People wearing summer clothes in the winter and winter clothes in the summer, swollen ankles and sneakers with the heels cut off to make them fit. Tired young mothers and worn-out old mothers, baby carriages, wheelchairs and walkers, hung-over old men and drunk young men, faces with foreign features, the smell of cabbage and garlic, vodka, urine, and layers of sweat dried into filth.

No one in the line has eyes, they all look away. Many of them have turned their faces to the wall or covered them from passing gazes with hoods and scarves. Many of them are wearing sunglasses even though the day is overcast.

I don't have the heart to say what they're waiting in line for. It's one of the city's shared secrets.

Today the line is particularly quiet and grim. The people in it avoid looking around.

I had nearly passed by, when one of the women in the line, maybe second or third from the front, struck me as familiar. I looked back and saw a forehead, a slender nose that I knew well, cheeks still round and unwrinkled.

Impossible! I had to be mistaken. But there I was, in broad daylight, seeing that pretty face with my own eyes. It was her, Viveca, my old classmate. I had just seen her last week at a concert of the Helsinki Philharmonic Orchestra. She and her husband, a permanent under-secretary of state, had season tickets.

In school, Viveca was always the first to get the latest brand-name clothes. When she grew up, she started dressing only in black and white. It was known that she had two cars, one white, the other black.

Today she had broken her routine. She was wearing a blue quilted jacket and a brown, fuzzy woollen hat. They didn't look like Viveca's own clothes, more like a costume. She turned and suddenly had eyes. I know she saw me—I saw the flash of recognition behind the mascara of her eyelashes. She made no move to greet me, just the opposite—she bent over to rummage through the bag at her feet. It was certainly Viveca's own, no ordinary shopping bag, but an elegant designer label, genuine leather. That bag confirmed her identity to me.

I got the message: she wanted me to move on, and I did.

My heart raced in my chest as if I had had a serious fright. "I'm going, I'm going," I whispered to myself. I stopped two blocks away, in front of the window of a thrift store. There was a sign in the window, "Closed due to a heart attack." I felt like I was having one as well.

Did Viveca stand in that line regularly, or was this a one-time experiment? She must have been standing there for a long time to make it all the way to the front. Maybe she had been commissioned to write an article about the line for some paper and she wanted to imbue it with extra authenticity by pretending to be one of its beneficiaries? But what paper would commission her to write an article? It didn't seem likely. As far as I knew, Viveca had never been a skilled writer, nor had any interest in being one.

Sometimes foreign organisms are found in places where they don't belong and can't survive. A jaguar in a suburban forest, a giant frog in the footwear section of a department store, a *Carcharodon megalodon* in the cholera basin. But this was a person who was completely out of place. Her presence was more than a mistake. It was indecent, practically a crime.

KINKY NIGHT

"Here's your ticket," the Marquis said one day and shoved a piece of paper at me.

"A ticket for what?" I asked and took a closer look at the paper. It was a ticket to the Kinky Club's Industrial Fairy Tale with Fetish Science Fiction.

"I want a short article on the city's kinky scene," he said.

"You go then," I said. "I don't feel like it."

The Marquis had suggested at many editorial meetings that *The New Anomalist* should start a column for deviant sex, or at least that we should publish something on the subject every now and then. "We have to expand our readership," he insisted. "When something stops growing, it withers away," he would say. I was of the opinion that branching out in that direction would actually drive away part of our readership.

The Marquis didn't listen, of course. And so I found myself at my first and last kinky night, watching a cabaret titled *Glam HC Sex Industrial*. To be completely honest, maybe I was a little curious about what was in store.

The young audience was dressed in black costumes decorated with shining metal. The only colors in sight were their red, blue, and green hairdos.

On stage, a man—I'm sorry, in this context the correct word is slave—was sucking the toes of a tattooed woman. It went on and on. The woman gyrated and made small, supposedly erotic noises as the man slurped on each toe in turn. I got extremely bored, and I thought that the slave and his mistress must also be eager for the performance to end. I was sorry I hadn't brought the Voynich manuscript or my knitting with me.

Once the toe-sucking had been completed, the woman urinated on her slave. He drank it. This elicited resounding applause from the audience and recaptured my attention.

Had I had my knitting with me, I might have felt like one of the *la tricoteuse*, the women who would sit by the guillotine knitting during the French revolution. I remember reading that in the Nazi concentration camps, the most sadistic guards served the same drink as one of their fiendish methods of torture. And now people were paying to watch it being gulped down on stage and applauded.

I was already very uncomfortable when a woman in a white thong walked on stage artfully twirling a shining knife. She had a slave, too, this one a girl. The woman cut a heart into the skin between the slave girl's naked breasts. Blood trickled, and the "torture" continued with more cuts to the stomach and buttocks.

More people came on stage dressed in spiked collars like badly behaved dogs and Loogaroo. Disgusted, I watched as they pierced each others' nipples and genitals to their hearts' content. Spiked clubs and other equally inappropriate objects were attached to sensitive places, but the climax was yet to come. The audience really came alive when one of the men set himself on fire. As the flames rose, I heard cries and squeals from the audience, not of horror, but of pleasure.

At this point, I finally got up and left. I had never felt older or colder than at that show. I had no intention of writing a single word about it. I sent a message that same night to the Marquis that he could forget about sending me to investigate any more industrial sex.

That night I ground up three datura seeds and ate them quickly with yogurt. I felt I needed them.

PHONY MONEY

I was reading a book on the tram. It had a peculiar title: *The Origin of Consciousness in the Breakdown of the Bicameral Mind*. I was completely absorbed in my reading, and when I lifted my eyes from the book, the city blocks I saw from the tram window were completely unfamiliar to me, and I realized that I'd missed my stop.

Had it been a new neighborhood, the sight wouldn't have surprised me. I hadn't wandered much outside of my familiar territory for the past few years, and many new neighborhoods had been built during that time.

But the buildings I saw from the tram were old. As far as I could tell, even the newest ones were from the 1920s. There were deteriorating low wooden houses here and there along the streets. I had thought that there were only a couple of buildings like that left in the city, preserved as museums. Sheets were hung out to dry in the yards of the wooden houses. The bare branches of overgrown lilacs protruded through picket fences. I couldn't remember ever having seen such yards or such a neighborhood.

"Excuse me," I asked the elderly lady sitting next to me, "where is this tram going?"

"Back to the railway station," she said.

"But the nine hasn't come this way before," I said.

She gave me a funny look.

"It has as long as I can remember."

"Excuse me," I said again, got up, and hopped out at the next stop. I was curious. I had to be somewhere east of the city center. I tried to look for the shore, but it was nowhere in sight. The streets were lined with small stores, grocers, and old-fashioned general goods stores.

For some reason, my gaze was drawn to the window of one of the stores. I saw a fruit basket and a box of Turkish delights that I had a sudden craving for. All of my attention was focused on that box. I felt as if, long ago, in my childhood, a visiting relative had given me just such a box of candy. My surroundings faded from sight, as if I had suddenly developed tunnel vision. Greed moved me towards the door to the store. I took out a largish bill from my wallet. I was sure it would be enough.

I stepped into the store, which had a vintage coffee advertisement on the wall.

"I'd like to buy that box in the window there," I said to the saleswoman. "How much does it cost?"

"Seven marks," she said, an old, dry woman with dozens of long pins in her hair.

I gave the woman my only bill. She turned it in her hands with a confused look. Then she brought it to her nose and sniffed it. Eventually she leveled a stern gaze on me.

"What kind of money is this then?" the woman asked.

"What do you mean what kind of money," I asked, confused. "It's a fifty, you can see that."

She didn't respond. Her eyes moved from me to the bill and back again. I began to lose my temper.

"It's legal tender, not a forgery."

"Not in this country it isn't," she said. "Don't you have any real money?"

"Are you joking?" I asked, flustered. I was getting hot under the collar, and I started to sweat. "It's a fifty, you must be able to see that, and you said the box is just seven marks. So give me forty-three marks change."

"You can keep your money," she said, "and I'll keep the candy. Or do you want me to call the police?"

"What on earth is going on?" I asked in a panic. I wasn't just asking the woman, but myself as well.

She didn't answer, just stared at me even more sternly than before and held out my bill between her thumb and forefinger as if it were contaminated.

I felt a twinge of fear. I could see that she was serious. But what had I done wrong?

I snatched my bill from her hand, completely perplexed, and left the store. I walked quickly, hardly looking to either side, distressed by what had just happened and almost expecting someone to be following me.

I was walking briskly, but the view to my side, which I only sensed faintly, seemed to change even more quickly, as if I were sitting in a speeding car. The next time I looked around me, I recognized the neighborhood and my city. I began to regain my composure.

At that moment I was approached by a bag lady, a habitual beggar. She is a fixture in the city. Threadbare, diminutive, and of an ethnic minority, she spends her days near the railway station and in front of downtown restaurants. For some reason, I find her intensely repulsive, and never give her any money.

Now she was approaching me with money in her hand. She had a bill in her hand, and wasn't asking me for anything. Just the opposite: she was trying to get me to take it! How strange and upside down! Wrong, completely wrong. Was she mocking me, or did she really think I needed the proceeds from her begging? Did I look so bad already?

Shouldn't I have at least thanked her for the offer? I didn't. I stepped aside quickly and irritably, raised my hand defensively, and I know my face was twisted by a grimace.

It wasn't until I had gotten past her that I realized that the incident was a kind of mirror of what had just happened in that strange store.

I couldn't get the woman or the phony money out of my head until, at the market square, a flock of pigeons rushed past me like a fountain, spreading into the air like the light gray seeds of a dandelion.

Those despised and persecuted birds, called flying rats by some, are masters of vertical flight. I admire them. The streets are like rock-hemmed canyons to them. The flare of movement, the beating of wings against smoke and air…

My thoughts rose with the pigeons to land on the eaves, antennas, chimneys, window ledges. There I left them, among the golden rows of lit windows.

A Finger

Raikka talks so much and so well about so many subjects and he isn't even out of school yet! The boy knows so much: superclusters and the structure of the universe, which is apparently filled with holes like Swiss cheese, the gradual increase of Uranus's apparent magnitude, infrared and asymmetrical galaxies. He can give entire lectures on strange radio pulses and vast bubbles, gamma ray bursts, the Omega Point, supermassive stars, and the sudden, sporadic cessation of radiation.

Raikka has already written several articles for *The New Anomalist* that have gotten a great deal of attention. He sounds like a poet when he talks about the pale blue glow of distant galaxies and the existence of vast vacuums. When the expansion of the universe accelerates, he said once, when all the heavenly bodies grow ever more distant ever more quickly, the universe will become ever emptier, colder, darker. It didn't seem to bother him, though.

He is an amateur of the highest order.

On the second day, he started talking about elementary particles. How taus breeze through the Earth lighter than any other particles, how they spill through us as if we were nothing.

"They have no charge," he said. "They weigh—if that verb can be used at all about them—only a millionth of the mass of an electron. Somewhere along their journey, they become leptons, which vanish in an instant.

"Try to think of a being that sees differently to us, say, with radio waves," Raikka once said. "That being would see the metal structures of buildings, but not the masonry, wood, or glass. It wouldn't see us, either, except for maybe our fillings. To a creature like that, we would be just pieces of metal floating in mid air.

"Did you know that dark matter is invisible, but most of the universe is made of it?" He asked me. "It could be the gravity of other, parallel universes. Light particles can't travel from one dimension to another. But gravity permeates everything."

That winter I felt gravity more clearly than ever before. One morning, as I sat at my desk in the office, depressed, with a jug of water in front of me, Raikka walked in. He asked for more time to finish the article about hole teleportation he was working on. His left middle finger was wrapped in gauze, and the boy looked dispirited and pale.

"Were you in an accident? What happened to your finger?"

"Nothing really. The tip was amputated, that's all," Raikka said.

"That sounds pretty bad! Lucky it was the left hand," I said to comfort him. "Does it ache? What happened?"

"Nothing serious," the boy said. "I stopped by the amputation parlor yesterday."

"Parlor?"

"Yeah, don't worry about it. It didn't cost much. It aches a little, but it'll be good as new soon. Well, shorter, obviously."

"I'm not following you," I said. "Don't tell me...dear God, the amputation was voluntary? You *paid* to have it done?"

"Well, it's not like professionals work for free. It's like you've never heard of this before. Everyone is getting it done these days."

"Everyone! I certainly haven't ever heard of such a thing before. Do you mean to tell me that there was nothing wrong with your finger?"

"Don't you get it? What would be wrong with it? It was a completely normal finger."

"But what was done to it isn't normal," I managed to say. "I'm reporting this. This is a matter for the police, a crime. Professionals do this, you say? Criminals, I call them!"

"They have all the licenses. It's a perfectly clean place."

I fell silent from shock and stared at his bandaged stump. Then I lost my temper.

"Get out," I said. "I've never heard of anything so perverse. And here I thought I knew everything there is to know about anomalies. This entire city is just one big anomaly. Amputation parlors! Drinking urine on stage! People setting themselves on fire!"

"What are you yelling for?" Raikka said. He had begun to look miserable as well. "I don't get it—it's not like it was your middle finger. And the tip isn't even necessary. You can't do anything much with your left middle finger anyway," he argued.

"Oh no? I'll show you what you can do with it!"

And I did.

"See? This is a human middle finger extended to its full length, fingernail and all. And that's how it's going to stay until it gets buried with the rest of me."

Raikka ran off. I think I had offended him to the core. He was still practically just a child. And how his amputated finger must have ached!

That ache lodged itself in my chest. It was so bad that I had to lie down on the mat for a while. It wasn't healthy to get so worked up. I was also sad that *The New Anomalist* had probably lost a good contributor. I doubted that Raikka would write any more articles for us on cosmology or the latest trends in alternative physics.

I wanted to say to him, "How could you, who knows everything there is to know about the gradual increase of Uranus's apparent magnitude, infrared and asymmetrical galaxies, who talks like a poet about the pale blue glow of distant galaxies and the vastness of vacuums, how could you of all people go and have the end of your left middle finger removed?"

Would he answer, "So that people wouldn't think I'm so weird..."?

Raikka was gone, but I remembered the lonely taus he had told me about, the taus that wander through our city, through amputation parlors and kinky parties and innovation centers at nearly the speed of light, hardly affecting anything, probably hardly affected by anything.

Trillions of them flow through our muscles and fat, our blood and our hard skulls. Then nothing meets nothingness. Nothing happens, and yet does happen. Nothing exists, and yet, something does.

The Moving Image of Eternity

"Everything that is large was once small. Even the universe was once small, smaller than the period at the end of a sentence," he said. "But that was before time and space. On the other hand, how can anything be called small, if there's nothing larger than it, if there's no one to see the smallness? And who could possibly be outside the universe?"

"Some people would say God," I said.

"But would anything be large or small to God? Actually, the universe was not a point, but a hole, it was a non-thing. When it stopped being a non-thing and became a thing, time can be said to have been born. Time, a shadow that eternity throws on the wall of our cave. Plato, you remember, 'the moving image of eternity'…"

He was an expert on time. I called him the Timely Man. There was once a menswear store called that in this city, at the beginning of time…

Where did I read this sentence? "We live in the hour all free of the hours gone by." It's rarely true, because we so rarely live in the moment: more often we live in our time.

When I was a child, when there was still a store called Timely Man in the city, I would experiment with time. I wanted to know how long the present lasts and what the present really is. I came to the conclusion that it can never last longer than a second or two. I tried so hard to hold on to the present with my eyes and ears, with all my attention, but before I realized, it had already slipped into the past.

It is impossible for us to hold back the flow of time, to be really present, to stretch out the moment without it tearing. Something always happens to break our concentration and push us into the uproar of the events around us.

I dress myself in time first thing in the morning—I wrap a watch around my wrist. Even while sleeping I'm troubled by the bustle of life. But that winter, I began forgetting appointments and meetings. I was supposed to go listen to the Timely Man's lecture at the Institute of Spiritual Growth and meet him afterwards. But even though I had marked the time and place in my calendar and though I thought I'd checked my schedule, I forgot the appointment. There were days when I couldn't remember what season it was without checking the newspaper.

And so, the Timely Man waited for me that day in the Institute's café. I didn't remember the appointment until the Marquis asked me how the interview had gone, and then I was alarmed.

"It's a pity you made him wait for nothing, a busy scholar. What's the matter with you?" the Marquis asked. "You seem so absent-minded and tired these days. Has your asthma gotten worse?"

"No no, just the opposite, actually," I said. "It's better now. I'm trying a new remedy, you know, herbal. But it does make me drowsy sometimes."

I felt my lips sticking together, and took a long sip from my water bottle. The Marquis stared at me suspiciously.

"I think you've lost weight. You should get yourself looked at," he said. "By the way, have you started wearing perfume? There's a strange smell in the office."

"No, I don't wear any," I said, embarrassed. I realized I was carrying around the stench of datura.

The next day, the Marquis brought the Timely Man with him to the office after treating him to lunch at The Foxhole. I'd do the interview at the office while the Marquis took off again. I didn't have the courage to ask how lunch had been—I just hoped that the Timely Man considered the establishment picturesque. He looked with polite interest at the products in the parastore that the Marquis forced me to show him. I was happy that the Timely Man didn't go near enough the bookshelf to set off the rock 'n' roll fish.

The Timely Man had studied cosmology, received his doctorate early and with honors, and been given a tenured position at a respected university. But one of his classes had caused serious controversy, an academic scandal of sorts, after which he thought it best to resign. The Timely Man drifted out into fringe research, forced to lecture at institutions of questionable repute, and publishing articles in magazines and journals just like *The New Anomalist*. His lecture at the Institute of Spiritual Growth was called "The Possibility and Impossibility of Time Dimensions."

I was relieved that the Timely Man accepted my profuse apologies with such grace. In fact, it seemed like he couldn't wait for the chance to give another lecture. My notes from our meeting don't do him justice: they only touch on a couple of the thoughts he presented. He also talked about dualities, Maxwell's equations, and D-branes. Most of what he said was far over my head due to my limited understanding, poor education, and mental state that day. I'm sure there are people who would say that there's no point in trying to understand the Timely Man's opinions, because he had drifted out of the scientific community, into the large and motley congregation of independent thinkers. But in our meeting, he emphasized that more and more scholars were supporting similar positions.

"One could say—and it was actually already proven back in 1949—that the passage of time is just an illusion," he said. "You've heard of superstring theory, I'm sure."

"I'm sorry to say I haven't."

I've noticed that this is a phrase I've had to repeat over and over again in the company of various experts.

"Superstring theory claims that elementary particles are not points, but vibrating strings. According to the theory, we have ten dimensions of space, six of which are so compactified that we can't see them. But this theory has had to be abandoned. M-theory states that there are actually eleven dimensions. But then there is F-theory, which is the one I subscribe to."

"And what does F-theory maintain then?" I asked.

"It holds that there are a total of twelve dimensions in the universe, two of which are dimensions of time," he explained. "Usually, you see, it's thought that space can and must have many dimensions, but that time has just one."

"Do you mean that, according to F-theory, there is a dimension where time doesn't flow from the past into the future?"

"That, too. But I'm inclined to trust that this particular hypothesis tells us something more specific about the universe than previous ones."

"And so effect wouldn't actually come after cause, is that it? That would create some real trouble," I said. "Contradictions and paradoxes. The kind of science-fiction stuff that can't be taken seriously. I'm sorry if I'm expressing myself crudely."

"A paradox for us, in any case," he said. "There's no escaping that."

"But if one could undo what has been done…"

"To us, time means always being carried, whether speeding or crawling, in the same direction, which we call the future. Every moment we leave the past behind us, in a place we cannot return to, whereas in space, we can move forward and backwards, up, down, and side to side. But if there is another dimension of time—as there is every reason to believe—we could also move diagonally…"

"Meaning…?"

"We could step aside when threatened by an unpleasant event…"

"…like death?" I blurted out.

"Yes, like death, for example," he agreed. "Or, if the need were to arise, we could retreat, loiter, stay in place, or charge forward, just as if time, too, had its own landscape and geography. We might to some extent be able to choose our pasts, because information could also travel from the future to the past."

"But how could we access such a dimension?"

"Well, that's the hard part. In this universe, at least."

"That's knowledge that humankind could really use. I mean, it would change everything. It could solve nearly all our problems."

"I wouldn't bet on that," he said. "Would it help us? Would we live our lives any more wisely? And if we didn't have shared time, would we even be living in the same world?"

"Yes," I admitted, "maybe it would actually lead to deeper unhappiness than ever before, chaos and unheard of agonies. What if everyone decided not to die, how would there be room for anyone new to be born?"

"It's entirely possible," the Timely Man said, "that we'll never have an alternative direction for time. It's possible that each universe has a unique combination of dimensions of time and space…Let me show you."

The Timely Man asked for some paper and began drawing diagrams. His verbose explanations were lost on me completely.

All I could take in was his voice, not what he said. Suddenly, in the company of this stranger, I was overcome with sympathy. Though I was looking past him and his papers, into the hazy cold of the winter day, I saw him as a being of time, and I saw myself as one as well. I could see him lengthen and thin out and lose his identity.

How deeply people put out roots into the place that becomes time. His beginning is as far away as mine, in the misty birth of the species and beyond, in the gaseous clouds of newly forming stars. The Timely Man is long as a sounding line, as a fishing line sinking into precipitous depths of unknown matter, the darkness of light years.

The beginning is so very far away, I thought, but the end is always near. That's what time means, to humans.

The Old Woman Ahead of Me

I see that old woman nearly every day now. I flinch when I see her walking ahead of me, always ahead of me. I've never yet caught a glimpse of her face.

A rosy scalp shows through her silvery white hair, carefully curled, but quite thinned already. She looks fragile and stooped, clearly very old. That considered, it's amazing how quickly she walks. She can keep up the same pace block after block. And how admirably certain and determined her movements are! She never hesitates at crossings, she seems to know where every street leads. She must have lived in this city a long time, decades, perhaps all her life.

I've followed her a couple of time, just to see where she's going. I've tailed her, spied on her, I'm ashamed to say. But I have nothing to show for it.

What a strange old woman! There is something eerie in the whole phenomenon. Whenever I take it upon myself to follow her, I soon lose sight of her in the swarming crowd. I can't keep up with her at all. Just when I think I've managed to get alongside her, she'll turn in toward a metro station and the escalators will whisk her out of my sight, or she'll duck into the revolving doors of a department store. I'll follow her to the cosmetics department, where people are listening to the product demonstrator's gospel, but all I'll see are adolescent girls, young women, and middle-aged women. She'll have lost me again.

Sometimes I try to be clever and rush down a side street to be able to walk down the boulevard in the opposite direction and come face to face with her. But when I turn, out of breath, onto the boulevard, the old woman is nowhere to be seen. I'm left standing, baffled, in front of a shop window containing disembodied legs dressed in this season's pantyhose.

A day or two will pass, and once again I'll see the old woman's back. As I step in one door of the café, she'll be stepping out the other. As I step down from the tram, she'll be climbing aboard. I finally found her standing still one day on my way back from the bank. She had stopped at the corner, waiting at the crosswalk as the traffic lights shone red for pedestrians. There she was—I was sure I'd finally catch her!

But as her thin neck was nearly in front of me, and her silvery curls almost tickled my nose, the light changed. She crossed the street at a run, but I stumbled. I made my way slowly, as if the air around me had thickened into a dense and sticky substance. A tram hid her from view for a moment, and when it had passed, the old woman had pulled her disappearing act again.

Frustrated, I swore, "Don't think you've gotten away. I'll catch you yet, and we'll meet each other face to face!"

The Mouse, the Wolf, and the Nightingale

This spring, before putting anything in the trashcan in the cupboard under the sink, I knock on the cupboard door. Is anyone home?

I know it's a very odd thing to do, but it serves a purpose. The cupboard is inhabited, at least from time to time. There is hole under the kitchen counter that the drainpipe disappears down. A mouse uses the hole to get to the delicacies in my trashcan. I knock on the cupboard door to warn the rodent. I don't want to catch it off guard— nor do I want to be caught off guard myself, unpleasantly startled to see it leap out of the trashcan when I open the door.

Have you heard of the black mouse and the white mouse? One is night and the other is day, but they both have the same job.

During the spring nights, I wake up in my bedroom to the mouse's rustling, whether it's the same mouse or a different one, I don't know. It's past midnight, but spring is already so far along that night isn't properly dark anymore, just a hazy twilight that dissolves color and blurs outlines. Daybreak is a while off; it's still the hour of the wolf, the hardest time of day for the children of man.

During the hour of the wolf, people are at their most defenseless. Their body temperature and energy levels are at their lowest, and their exhaustion is at its deepest. But the mouse nibbles and labors away. One couldn't be blamed for thinking that a thief had broken in to do his sly work. And it is a thief, stealing my life. The black mouse always works the nightshift. Its associate, the white mouse, does its work during the day. I just can't make out its rustling in the incessant clamor of the day. Now it's the black mouse's turn to gnaw through my life's thread, no, the umbilical cord through which life nourishes me. That is the job of the black mouse, and also the white.

But at the same time, from the thicket of bird cherry and black alder in the park, I hear the melody of a nightingale—the last of the evening or the first of the morning? Such energy, such joy tinkling in the twilight, the boundary between night and day. An invisible fountain of volition and hope leaping into the air, glistening in the spring landscape. The nightingale is a different time. It doesn't live in the hour of the wolf.

> "Earth and sky, forest, and fallow-plot,
> Caught that discontinuous strain,
> Those portionings out by lot
> Of trials, glee, fatuities, and pain."

I'm awake now, at least almost, and listening to two sounds at the same time, the mouse and the nightingale. Hearing connects me to both the indoors and the out. I can hear the nearness, and I can hear the distance. I can hear the infiniteness of space. My senses give me both myself and that which is not me. They are both a bridge and a chasm. When they disappear, I suppose I will disappear as well.

It's night for all of us now, the mouse, the nightingale, and me, their audience. But it's not the same moment; each of us has our own. I alone, at least so I believe, am the only thing connecting our moments. Or could the mouse, between nibbles, be listening to the nightingale's song? That is all I am now, a listener of the sound made by these two. One is nibbling away inside, the other singing outside. Both completely unaware of their audience.

Suddenly, still half asleep, I understand: the mouse truly is inside, inside me. It lives in me, they live in me and always have, the day mouse and the night mouse both. They are a part of me, a temporal being who is shortened by each passing day and night.

But the nightingale trills in mists of dawn, outside of me, in the real spring. There is another reality out there, in which I, too, have gone about my business, but only part of me. Was it only my ears that flew

128

there? Is everything else left here, with the mouse, in the hour of the wolf?

And I say to the mouse, "Gnaw away, do the work that was given to you, that you were born to do. It won't be long before the thread is severed. What then? The nightingale's song is something you cannot chew through, mouse. The song is also an umbilical cord, still feeding me with wordless melodies. There will come a time when I can no longer hear your nibbling or the nightingale's song. But as long as I remember the nightingale, I will believe in eternity, I will believe that there is no end to spring, or to me.

It's always spring somewhere. There is always someone to hear the nightingale's song.

And I fall asleep again to song and nibbling and to the smell of datura. My dream, reality! Now the building in which the mouse is nibbling is within me, but so is the city, the nightingale's park, and further away, the harbor, the open sea, the sky. They are all in me, part of me, and I am gone.

The Third Seed Pod

Madame Maya

I began to hear a thumping. The potted orchid on the window sill trembled. The floor shook and my pen rolled off my desk. I was startled, and when I saw her, I was startled again.

What a lady! She must have weighed three hundred thirty or even three hundred fifty pounds. She puffed and panted as she lumbered into our cramped office in her red rubber boots. The weather wasn't rainy, so maybe boots were the only kind of footwear she could squeeze on to her swollen feet. The legs of her boots were slit open, and the fat on her legs forced her to walk with her legs apart. Her features, which perhaps could have once been called beautiful, were obscured by her sagging jowls and multiple chins.

She, too, was one of the magazine's loyal subscribers. She said she wanted to discuss a certain interesting phenomenon.

"Have you noticed," she asked after waddling around the room for a moment examining all of the available seats and finally settling in the armchair I had bought at the flea market, which cried out in distress under her weight. "That sometimes, in a certain light, usually at nightfall, matter can become partially transparent?"

"No I haven't," I said, surprised. It was an unconventional start to a conversation, to say the least.

"But it does," she insisted.

I glanced at her fingers and looked quickly away. She wasn't wearing any rings, and even bracelets would have pressed into her fat fingers, which probably always stuck out in slightly different directions. The folds of flesh around her wrists spilled over the armrests of the chair.

I had never met this lady before. I had actually already closed the office for the day, but had come back for my transcription of the

Voynich manuscript, which I planned to continue parsing at home. I had left the door ajar, and she had crammed herself into the hallway before I noticed.

It wasn't only her size that drew attention, but also her outfit. Her windbreaker, adorned with long-faded violet and orange stripes, hung open. Her huge bust made it impossible to close the zipper. Beneath the coat, she wore some kind of sweatshirt that was the color of grass.

Her voice boomed from the depths of a mountain of flesh, low like a man's.

"I would like to talk to you about this phenomenon and ask whether you are perhaps already aware of it or have yourself had similar experiences."

"This is the first I've heard of it," I said cautiously. "When you say matter becomes transparent, what kind of matter do you mean?"

"Human flesh, for example," she said. "If the conditions are right, I can see objects through my arm."

I didn't really know what to say to that. Her arms filled in the sleeves of her windbreaker to the point that they had started coming apart at the seams. Arms like that did nothing to help the credibility of her claim.

"Your bare arm?" I asked just for the sake of it. "If you're dressed, do you also see through your sleeve?"

"Through the sleeve as well, of course," she said.

"And what kind of objects do you see through your arm and sleeve?" I asked, getting more and more confused.

"Whatever happens to be around," she said with a snort, or a sound more like a motor turning over. She looked amused. I realized how stupid my question had been and felt embarrassed.

"I don't generally go looking at things through my arm," she explained patiently. "At the right moment, any material—wood, metal, stone—can become transparent. Locked doors, the walls we live within, anything can turn into gauze, and you can see the world through it like through a dusty window, like the one you have here," she said and pointed at the window at the top of our wall.

"Well, that sounds...sounds quite remarkable," I said without much enthusiasm.

"But matter *is* a remarkable phenomenon," she said. "We think we understand it, but it always surprises us."

"Don't you think that it's more a question of you having a special ability than a quality of matter itself?"

"If I have this gift of sight, then everyone else does as well," she said forcefully. "It's just that not everyone is able to use it. It's latent in them. But if and because everyone has this ability, doesn't that mean that matter is something completely different than what we imagine? And light, too, because this obviously also has to do with the characteristics of light. A certain wavelength, field effects, who knows."

"That bears thinking about," I said.

"It's important. Think about it and look around," she said.

"Would now be an opportune time by any chance?" I asked.

"No, now is not the right time," she said and looked past her cheeks to the window pane, beyond which the day was already fading.

"The light is still too glaring. One has to wait until the evening cools and the light falls at an angle. It doesn't happen every evening, though. Humidity is also a factor, cloud altitude and density, special atmospheric conditions. I haven't yet figured out all the necessary parameters. I'll be sure to let you know once I've gotten a little further in my research."

She said this with a dignified nod that shook all her chins, as if this were actually an academic branch of science.

"But start keeping an eye out today. Be observant. You may not succeed in the first weeks or even months. But the right day will come, and then you'll see…

"Just think," she said, swaying in her seat, "What we call matter is just a dance of elementary particles. And it's a long way from one particle to the next. And all these particles are invisible. Isn't the strange thing actually that we don't automatically see through everything all the time?"

"You're right about that," I said, and a new thought occurred to me. "But isn't it even stranger that we see anything at all, if there isn't actually anything to see?"

"It's all the veil of maya," she said and heaved her majestic tonnage from the chair.

Did she actually say that, or was it me? How heavy a veil can be, I thought while watching her heaving and panting flesh traverse the room, disturbing things along the way.

Oh madame, wherever you are, do you still drag the weight of your own veil?

CAKE

Do you remember how we only met once that year, in September? I was in a bookshop downtown looking for a book called *Towards Robot Consciousness* when I noticed your profile in the newspaper section. You were leafing through some foreign daily. There had been a serious plane crash the day before, which was suspected to be part of a coup, and I thought maybe you were looking for news about it. You didn't seem particularly happy to see me. In fact, I would have just walked quietly by had you not happened to look up from your paper at that exact moment. We agreed to have coffee upstairs, in the book café, where they have particularly good cappuccino and end-of-the-world cake: chocolate confections decorated with a marzipan skull.

We traded news. You told me you had gotten divorced, taken out a large mortgage, and recently moved into a new apartment. You were able to, because you'd just gotten a senior researcher's position at the Academy of Finland. I congratulated you. I told you a bit about *The New Anomalist*, but our conversation soon sputtered out. We were both a bit uncomfortable. It had been a long time since we had sat together, just the two of us.

Someone had left a magazine on our table.

You began leafing through it and said, "Aha! Here's the article I've been looking for. The one by Huntington on the clash of civilizations."

"Don't let me stop you, go ahead and read it," I said.

You buried your head in the magazine, and I reluctantly spooned end-of-the-world cake into my mouth. My appetite had almost completely disappeared that year. Instead, I asked the waitress for another glass of water. I had a burning thirst, as I always did back then. What had been my favorite dessert no longer pleased me, I was downhearted, unhappy with myself. Why couldn't I carry on a conversation with my old friend?

Suddenly, without lifting your eyes from the magazine, you said, "Apropos, the old woman who walks so extraordinarily quickly..."

I was too surprised to say anything. You still weren't looking at me, your eyes firmly on your magazine. Your mouth didn't even seem to move when you said, "Don't hurry too much. Don't try to catch up with her. You don't have to. She will catch up with you, of that you can be sure. Sooner than you think."

How could he know about her?

Stubbornly reading your magazine, you went on, "You must know who the old woman really is. The future is terrifyingly fast, always overtaking us. It only looks like it's ahead of us. In reality, it's pursuing us. It's a predator."

I was beginning to get irritated and said, "You know, I think I had better leave. You're having some strange thoughts today. Where on earth did you get them?"

You seemed to wake up then and finally lifted your gaze.

"Sorry, what was that? This Huntington can really write, though I don't necessarily agree with everything he has to say. You should give it a read, too."

When we were standing on the escalator, I asked, "Why did you say what you did just then?"

"Why did I say what?"

"About the old woman."

I was becoming more and more insecure.

"When?"

"In the café."

"In the café? I'm sorry, I'm not quite sure what you mean. We didn't talk about any old women. I lost myself in the magazine, and before that we talked about my new apartment and your new job."

That's what you said, and I was left alone with my disbelief. The end-of-the-world cake's sugary flavor lingered on my tongue. Either my friends were lying to me, or I was being betrayed by my own senses.

THE SOUND SWALLOWER

The office doorbell rang just as I was trying to finally finish my article about the Voynich manuscript. Or did I mishear? I often found my ears ringing these days. I tried to focus only on the real, like Ursula had advised me to. Perhaps someone had rung the bell on their bicycle on the street outside. I couldn't be bothered to get up, and turned my attention back to the manuscript:

a.K. ₰ſ₰. то. ɒто. тӈ2о₁. оӈаR.

But then I heard another ring—the doorbell after all—and I had to get up to answer it.

There he was again, quiet and dressed in a gray suit, the Master of Sound, the one with an interest in alternative audio technology. He had with him a backpack that didn't suit the rest of his attire, and he proceeded to carefully place it on the floor.

"I happened to remember while I was passing by," he said, "that you had mumblemumble about the Detector of Silent Sounds. Remember?"

I admitted that I did remember.

"Is your article ready?" I asked.

"Not yet, unfortunately. You see, I've been spending my time developing a mumblemumble. I have it with me. I've been working on it for a while, and I've got it working in a mumblemumble way.

Maybe you'd like a demonstration."

"What is it?" I asked.

"It's a mumblemumble swallower."

"A sound swallower?"

"Precisely. Its operational mumblemumble is almost the mumblemumble of the Detector of Silent Sounds, the device I told you about last time. When you hold the Sound Swallower to your ear, distracting sounds mumblemumble."

I held the gadget in my hands, looking at it from various angles. It didn't look like much. It couldn't really be called a machine at all. It was a quite tall, lidless cardboard cylinder, probably used to hold tea. It had been packed tight with plastic straws, blue and red and yellow, the kind normally used at children's birthday parties.

I lifted it up to my ear. There was a murmur. The effect was similar to holding a large conch shell to one's ear.

"Wouldn't earplugs be more practical," I asked. "And shouldn't these come in pairs? But then you'd have to tape them to your head."

"Well, this is a protomumble," he said. "There's room for development."

I remembered that, as a young student, I had spent a couple of months in an unfamiliar town living in a dorm that was next to the town's busiest intersection. There was an emergency services station across the street from the dorm, and ambulances and fire trucks would howl off at all hours. I wasn't able to sleep. I was comforted by the thought of how thin the Earth's atmosphere is, only seven-and-a-half miles. Nothing more than a skin. How quickly all noises fade when rising just a bit higher.

And how soon they stop being heard altogether if one descends just a few inches beneath the surface, among the roots and the worms. It was then that I began to understand that sounds were an exceptional phenomenon, that silence and darkness were the normal state of the universe and that an infinite noiseless night surrounded all sounds and images. I thought that I should actually learn to celebrate every sound, even cacophonies. Even the howling of ambulances and fire trucks, which are heralds of catastrophe and mortal danger, but also of the fact that we are still alive.

Time and change have a voice; eternity is silent. The human ear is always searching for one or the other.

So I found myself saying, "I could use a Sound Swallower. How much do you want for it?"

"Oh, I hadn't thought of mumblemumble. But if you want it... Maybe mumblemumble."

"How much did you say?"

"Ten marks."

"Ten marks isn't much for silence."

"When I've finished the mumblemumble version, I'll bring it for you to try," the Master of Sound said.

I paid him, and he left. It was quiet again, but only for a moment. Then I heard humming in the entryway.

"Look at this," I said and handed the Marquis the instrument I had just purchased. I told him about its alleged effects.

The Marquis examined the Sound Swallower. He put it to his ear for a moment and looked thoughtful.

"Well, I can't say I notice any effect," he said. "But I think many of our customers would be excited. That man could start mass-producing Sound Swallowers. That would be something."

"I don't think so."

"Maybe you're right. On second thought, it might be smarter to expand into solar engines and aura cameras. I got hold of some brochures. Do you want to see? Another thing worth considering would be an N-Machine."

"An N-Machine?"

"Yes, or then a homopolar generator."

I didn't ask what they were or what they did. When the Marquis left, I climbed up on a stool to open the window. From the unseen heights of the sky, the first snow swirled, radiant, into the cone of the street light and fell onto the frozen puddle.

So early! I thought. My second datura winter had begun.

All matter has its sound, but the first snow has none. Its arrival showers silence on the land and brings with it eternity itself.

The Trepanist

If there's one *New Anomalist* subscriber who could be filed under stark raving mad, I'd have to say, with only the briefest of hesitation, that it would be the man we called Carl Gustav Cork. I only hesitate because I also became acquainted—though only via email—with a person who believed in reversed speech. The young lady in question believed that recording someone's speech and then playing it in reverse would reveal what that person really meant. I understood that she shared this conviction with an extensive group of people, if not an entire cult. Though a speaker knowingly lied, the young lady wrote, that person's secret motives could not help but be revealed. Reversed speech would uncover what a person most wants to hide.

But Cork was a much more serious case. There was an abandon and determination in him that made me shudder. For legal reasons, I'll let his identity remain a secret.

Cork had sent the magazine an extensive article entitled: "Enlightenment Through Trepanation!"

"What's trepanation?" I asked the Marquis, who happened to be in the office when I opened the letter.

He hadn't heard the term either. After reading the article, neither of us wanted to hear it again. For once, we agreed. We didn't publish the article. Even the Marquis thought it crossed the line of decency.

I was so infuriated by Cork's piece that I didn't even answer it with a short form letter as I usually would: "Thank you for your contribution, but unfortunately…"

Soon after the next issue had come out, a mountain of a man showed up at the office wearing an ugly hardware store baseball cap. He introduced himself as the author of the trepanation article and demanded to know why the article hadn't been published. I thought it was strange and impolite that he didn't take off his hat, but his reasons became apparent soon enough.

I decided to be as clear as I could.

"Because we cannot encourage our readers to do anything so foolish," I said. "We would probably be sued if we did, and so would you."

"Risks have to be taken," he said and stuck out his stout jaw. "When the benefit and well-being of mankind is in the balance, laws and conventions must be defied. Trepanation opens the human mind to vast new vistas. It is a procedure that breaks new ground for the spirit. It offers the chance to escape the prison of materiality represented by our ossified skulls."

"I'm not the least bit convinced by your theory," I said and turned my attention back to my papers. I hoped that he would take the hint and leave.

"It seems you haven't acquainted yourself enough with this matter," he accused. "Did you even read the entire article?"

I began to get angry.

"I am as acquainted with it as I need to be. You want people to drill holes in their own skulls. I think that's utterly irresponsible. Even lobotomies are punishable by law these days. They led to thousands of people being degenerated into imbeciles. The poor souls who were subjected to that abuse can now demand compensation for their suffering. You even give advice on what kind of drill people should use to perforate their skulls."

"Of course I do," the man said. "It's the most necessary of advice. Black & Decker is by far the best choice."

"You," I went on, "drew a comic strip illustrating how to go about drilling open one's own head. Your proposal is beyond the pale."

"Now listen here, you're obviously unaware that trepanation has met with great success for millennia. It is a noble skill. The ancient Greeks, Romans, Egyptians, and Indians all knew the secrets of trepanation, though they usually only performed it on slaves and the lower classes."

"I don't doubt that for a second," I said. "The history of humanity is one shameful chapter after another."

"In the middle ages, skulls were opened to let demons out. There is evidence that those who survived the operation gained new, even supernatural, spiritual abilities."

"And just how many survived, I wonder?"

"As people grow up, they lose their original intuition and fresh ability to observe the world," Cork continued, paying no attention to my question. "The flow of blood to the brain is reduced, perception and emotions become flat. It has been scientifically proven that trepanation restores vitality to the senses and potency to the emotions."

"Scientifically, you say," I mumbled.

He wasn't about to let me get in the way of his lecture.

"As you know, newborns have a fontanel in their skull that slowly closes up. Our skulls harden with age, the flow of blood ebbs. Trepanation is one of the most effective and permanent methods of restoring us to our original state of flexibility and happiness. I even know a doctor, a surgeon, who drilled a hole in his skull with an electric drill. He's never felt better! I can give you his name and address and you can ask him for details yourself."

"No thank you," I remained cold. He really looked like he meant to dig out a pen and paper.

"If you ask me, you have a duty to tell your readers about this procedure!"

His tone sharpened. He put both hands—and they were huge mitts—on my desk and leaned in so close that the brim of his cap brushed my forehead. The situation was getting uncomfortable, even threatening. I pushed my chair back farther from the table and wondered whether I should try to call the Marquis.

"My conscience will be clear even if I never mention your procedure to a soul," I assured him, but my voice came out weak and uncertain.

"Don't you want to hear about my experiences?" he asked.

"I'd rather not, thank you very much," I said.

But he didn't respect my wishes, and instead snatched the cap off his head and turned his back to me. I was flabbergasted. There before my eyes, amongst thinning gray hair, nearly in the center of the crown of his head, was a cork, an ordinary cork from a wine or perhaps a champagne bottle.

What would have happened had it been pulled out? I trembled as I imagined a wet pop, followed by the murky contents of his skull gushing into the room.

"I got benzocaine for a local anesthetic and various bandaging materials," he went on, replacing his cap. "Iodine is, of course, necessary for sterilizing the hole. I went to the hardware store and bought a light, high-quality hand drill and drill bits made for ceramic tile. I was disappointed with the service, though. I asked the salesman what kind of bit he would recommend for drilling into the skull. Can you imagine he said he really couldn't recommend anything? Such poorly trained employees! In the end, I was happy with my choice, though a bit made for drilling metal might also work. I absolutely recommend a double-handled Black & Decker."

I hoped that he would stop, and I began impolitely underlining my copy of the Voynich manuscript. But Cork leaned over my desk again, and I felt a heavy, sickeningly sweet waft of air. I shrank back in my chair. It could have been the stench of his cerebral fluids.

"It's best to use a chair with a head rest. A good office chair or a sturdy armchair would work fine. If you manage to borrow a dentist's chair, you can congratulate yourself. You will also have to build some kind of support, to keep your head absolutely still. And then a seatbelt, don't forget a seatbelt! It would be most unfortunate if the drill were to skip around here and there."

"Now listen, I'm quite busy at the moment," I said tiredly.

"I started drilling slow and easy with the help of a friend of mine who's dedicated to the cause," he continued. "In fact, I've promised to return the favor to him. Having observed the procedure, he is convinced of its benefits and can hardly wait for his turn."

I groaned and felt faint.

"The work progressed slowly, but the hole in my skull grew deeper and deeper, until after about an hour, I heard a new, extraordinary sound, like a kind of bubbling or fizzing. I realized what it was: air bubbles under my skull had been freed from their skeletal prison. What joy! My friend carefully pulled the drill out of the opening.

"I really don't want to hear any more," I said. I was afraid I'd throw up.

Despite my expressed disgust, this ruthless man went on: "With two mirrors, I was able to see the blood ebbing and flowing in the opening in time with my heartbeat. I felt euphoria, an unprecedented joy and peace of mind. That feeling has stayed with me ever since. How I wish that more people could experience it! You, too, my friend!"

He patted my arm.

"It isn't even expensive. I've already given lectures on the blessings of this procedure to many clubs and societies. I implore you, seize this opportunity and publish my article. It could bring quality and wellbeing to the dull lives of countless citizens. If enough people understand the benefits of this procedure, the fate of the entire nation could be changed! There must be a political party that would make this their banner issue."

I tried to collect myself and put some authority into my voice. "We are not publishing your article. It's completely out of the question! This is my final word. You can always self-publish if you're determined to get sued."

"I'm disappointed and astonished. I would have expected a bit more open-mindedness from *The New Anomalist*," he said, dissatisfied.

"I'm sorry," I said.

I was amazed that he finally seemed to give up hope of making me understand. Relieved, I showed him out, and I didn't like the look on his face when he said goodbye. It didn't look anything like euphoria to me.

"You'll regret this, madam," he said. "You are in dire need of trepanation. This isn't over."

I wondered whether Cork could have fit a double-handled Black & Decker in the pocket of his windbreaker. After that episode, at my insistence, the Marquis had a peephole installed in the office door.

TWO MARCHES

"Yeats was right," Kurt said. "The best lack all conviction, while the worst are full of passionate intensity."

Kurt himself certainly didn't lack conviction—some would say he had too much—but he was also a hot-blooded man, intense and passionate. He said that the state was the new Leviathan, spreading totalitarianism and violence. He was certain that big corporations are Beelzebubs, evil incarnate.

When I was a young student, an acquaintance accused me of being politically naïve. Maybe it was Kurt. He was probably right on the money. I confess, my social awareness was—and still is—poorly developed. I was attracted to flowers, poems, and the glowing images that wander in the dreaming darkness, not the complicated machine that we call society. My knowledge of the history of the nation, of warring ideologies and power relationships, was pathetic. I couldn't tell the difference between anarchists, Trotskyists, Maoists, and syndicalists. I couldn't be bothered to read up on the reasons behind famines and inequality, the unfairness of taxation, or the problems caused by development aid, unemployment, or free trade. Lines like "Roll on, thou deep and dark blue Ocean, roll!" inspired me more than exclamation marks painted on banners ever could.

Kurt was different, even back then. From his new home across the sea, he follows events in his homeland every day. He monitors the employment situation, stock market fluctuations, mergers, protests, and the fortunes of political parties. But more than what's happening now, he's fascinated by what is going to happen soon, very soon. He's always predicting revolutionary developments, radical changes.

"The government will fall any day now," he would say. "Big things are happening. This isn't kids' stuff anymore. You'll see. Things will really get going this spring!" (Or fall, or winter.)

For many weeks now, he had been waiting in that other country for protests to start here. Many radical groups were preparing a march to demand that civil liberties be secured and that concentrations of political power be dismantled. It was meant to start on the nation's great day of celebration.

"What do you think, how many people will join the march?" he asked me over the phone.

"Well, I really couldn't say," I answered. "Maybe fifty, maybe a hundred."

"If it's a hundred, the government will fall. You'll see, that's what will happen," Kurt assured me.

So what if it did, I thought. Even if it fell, how much would change? I would go on living just the same, minding my own business and lost in my own thoughts, reading the Voynich manuscript, listening to the Heretics, coughing, drinking gallons and gallons of water and tea.

"So much will change," Kurt went on. "A new era is dawning. Even those of conventional talent and average intellect are beginning to sense it."

He often spoke of conventional talents, people who were competent enough, but who lacked a deeper intuition and analytical mindset and who he felt a subtle contempt towards. No doubt I fell into that category, though he deigned to enlighten me patiently enough.

Kurt was impatient to board the ferry to home. He planned to take part in the protest, to see the triumphant march, to witness this momentous event in the history of his former homeland. But the day came and went. I had promised to meet Kurt at the square. The ship had landed at the eastern harbor early that morning. I waited and waited, but there was no sign of Kurt. There was no sign of the march either, but the chill wind blew a crumpled paper to my feet. I picked it up—I wasn't sure why—and was taken aback. It was a flyer for the protest I was waiting for. It said that the march would start an hour later than I had told Kurt. I was cold and sorry for my mistake. It began snowing, and I remembered Andersen's *The Snow Queen*, as I always do when it snows. I remembered the splinter in Kai's eye that made him so evil.

It was cold, and I ducked into a café on a side street to warm myself up with a couple of cups of bergamot-flavored tea.

When I stepped back out onto the street, I heard singing from another square and saw the light from torches. A march was just arriving there, but not the one Kurt and I were waiting for. This was no protest, but a ceremonious procession. The participants were singing of swords and shields, castles, and safety in a time of trials and danger. How could I have forgotten that this procession, traditional and patriotic, was also scheduled for today? How slowly and respectably they walked, torches spitting sparks into the wind, how upright, beautiful, and expensively dressed.

There was a man walking near the middle of the procession who stood almost a head taller than the others. He wore a yellowed student cap, under which I thought I saw familiar, spiteful features, a protruding jaw, and swollen cheeks. Could it be him, the trepanist? I thought I could even make out his gravelly voice among the other singers. The last time I'd seen him, he had been dressed completely differently and had been wearing a yellow hardware store cap. This man was carrying a briefcase, and I couldn't help but wonder whether he had a double-handled Black & Decker with him.

I turned away. I didn't want him to recognize me. The street I was standing on connected one square to the other. On my right, I heard patriotic hymns, on my left, the barking of dogs. Preparations were underway for the protest, the provocation. Riot fences had already been put up. Police patrols and police cars, silent helmeted men and well-trained canine units, awaited the marchers while snowflakes coated the square in silver.

At the end of the street, I could already see banners, balloons, and signs. Finally, the sounds of chanting, running steps, and a musical racket were carried on the wind. The march looked more like a cheerful carnival than a protest. Banners waved and bounced to the beat of bongo drums as they approached the square. Whistles hurried from block to block. Under the smoke-gray, frozen sky, over the black and gray and white of the streets, girls danced like a row of flowers, dressed in reds and greens. A boy with blue hair was banging on a plastic canister. An old woman was carrying a threadbare umbrella. The words SOCIAL SECURITY had been painted on it.

From a flimsy stage erected in the middle of the square, I heard the words, "A century of violent history is oppressing us like an evil ghost. The only ideology that remains is buying low and selling high. We need a return to sense, but when has sense ever commanded human history? Will we ever learn to control our actions? Will we ever learn to recognize the evil consequences of our good intentions?"

I was happy to listen. The man made sense, but as I listened, I remembered that I had an article on the gruesome fate of Countess Cornelia di Bandi to finish. Kurt would manage without me, if he had even come.

He called me in the evening.

"Where were you?" I asked. "Weren't you able to come? I'm sorry I gave you the wrong time."

"I was there."

His voice boomed strong and deep, almost enraptured. "And it was so beautiful! How solemn and noble a procession!"

His choice of words puzzled me. "Well," I said, "I guess you could call it beautiful."

"And the torches!"

"The torches?"

"Such poise, such order!" he went on in his excitement. "Such a procession was a joy to see. The relationship of the young intelligentsia is still alive and organic here! This kind of activism is delightful."

Then I understood. He had gone to the wrong march, but I didn't have the heart to tell him. He left the country that same evening, and the government failed to fall.

THE OTHERKIN

Of all the groups of people I came across in my years at *The New Anomalist*, the most eccentric were without a doubt the Otherkin. Loogaroo was one of them. Actually, I really shouldn't talk about a group of *people*. They call themselves Otherkin, because they don't consider themselves to be human. They are a different species, of a different origin. Their souls—and I apologize for having to once again use this questionable and contentious word—are not human souls. They consider themselves other beings, who for some reason just happened to wind up living in human bodies.

After I began using datura, I found it easier to relate to these kinds of stories and even these "people." Some called themselves interdimensional beings. For whatever reason—so they claimed—they had been cast from their own world into the territory of *Homo sapiens*. There are many kinds of these interstitial residents: gryphons, dryads, therianthropes, sidhe, fairies, demons, gnomes, nymphs, vampires, etc. There are also shapeshifters that change form in different situations, sometimes against their will.

Several of these beings had a close bond with a certain species of animal, such as lycanthropes with wolves. The soul of the animal is joined to their own. Others, like vampires and gnomes, have an affinity for darkness. They avoid daylight and are most lively at night.

Loogaroo mentioned these beings to me during our second conversation. She had read my interview after all, and even made a couple of corrections. This meeting was much friendlier than the first.

"Sometimes, switches occur while we sleep," Loogaroo said.

"Switches?"

"People sometimes wake up as a different person than what they were when they went to sleep. They will have the memories, past, body language, expressions, and language of a different person. They might not only wake up a different person, but a different species, a changeling. Only the body looks the same as before."

Loogaroo said that many of the Otherkin come from other worlds, *Elenari* worlds.

"Where are they?" I asked.

"Some are underground. Many different peoples live there," she claimed.

"I remember hearing," I said, "that an astronomer once claimed that the earth is hollow, like a Russian doll, and that there are many smaller, concentric earths within it."

"That's exactly how it is," she said. "Each circle is home to its own forms of life. Each sphere has its own atmosphere, which gives off a steady, permanent light. There is a solid core in the very center, like a nut, but much bigger, of course, about the size of Mercury."

"But all that," I tried to say, "has been proven false long ago."

"Some Otherkin are from these smaller earths," she continued, unfazed. "Then there are Otherkin that live in completely different dimensions, different universes. Humans rarely see these lands, though they are sometimes right next to us, strange universes just a few millimeters away. Sometimes a medicine can thrust a person into the wrong place, and sometimes people are kidnapped.

"But those worlds are not for humans, humans should not seek them out," Loogaroo said, non-human herself.

She looked at me with an inquiring gaze, as if she suspected something or wanted to warn me. That day, I almost believed that she had turned seventy long ago.

The Ghost of the City Office

I've never had a more politically incorrect acquaintance than Emmi
D. Despite her many virtues, Emmi D. was a social oaf, inflexible,
intolerant, in a word, insufferable.

Though the death of a contemporary and a classmate should never
leave one indifferent, I was less affected by Emmi D's death than I was
by the episode that followed it.

For twenty years, up to the day that she was hounded out, Emmi
D. held a post in the city office. I don't want to berate her colleagues,
though, despite the fact that Emmi D. was a friend of sorts—with the
emphasis on "of sorts"—and despite the fact that she performed her
work without reproach.

From time to time, the offspring of one of her colleagues would visit
the office needing to talk with their mother or father. If this youngster
took the liberty of greeting Emmi D. with the profane expression
"Hi!" and departing with an energetic "Bye!", this seemingly minor
event would lead to unexpected consequences. In such cases, Emmi
D. would approach the youngster's parent and ask, "Could I have a
few words with you?"

Then she would proceed to instruct the parent that it is the elder
person who greets first should they deem it appropriate, and only
then may the younger person respond. Naturally, even then, the
expression "Hi!" would be out of the question, as would be a "Bye!"
called out upon departure. Before noon, the proper greeting is "good
morning," and after noon, "good day." If one is unwilling to depart

with the austere and traditional expression "goodbye," an appropriate substitute would be "have a nice day."

After imparting this advice, Emmi D. would inform the parent that, as the person responsible for the youth's upbringing, he or she should shape up. If his or her offspring were to fail to learn decent manners in time, the child would most likely sooner or later take up a life of crime. "*Vestigia terrent*," Emmi would say. (She often liked using Latin expressions, at times in the entirely wrong context.)

I said that Emmi D. was a friend "of sorts." What sort of friend was she, then? Perhaps it would be better not to call our slowly evolved and in many ways superficial relationship a friendship. If someone were to ask me what we had in common and why I kept in touch with her over the decades, however infrequently, I wouldn't be able to give them a credible answer. I had met Emmi back in university, and her obvious eccentricity caught my attention. She walked as if always on tiptoe. Her skull was an uncommon shape, a fact from which an early twentieth Century phrenologist would have drawn far-reaching conclusions. Her features would probably have been called "degenerate."

I'm ashamed to admit that I observed her like a strange species of animal. I was puzzled by what made her act the way she did, persistently repeating the same pattern to her own detriment.

What our relationship meant to her, on the other hand, I never discovered. After our meetings, I was left feeling a mix of rage, amusement, and embarrassment, but the fact of the matter was that I was the one who kept in touch with her.

In my living room, over a low bookshelf, hung an oil painting depicting a jubilant crowd holding flowers and banners in a square. It was by a well-known artist friend of mine. I don't know why Emmi D. hated it so much, but every time she visited, she made a snide remark about it. I assume it was more a question of her disliking the artist. Emmi D. had only once met the artist when the artist was out on the street walking a dog, an old Airedale Terrier. Emmi never could stand dogs. After that, she always referred to the artist as "that dog person."

How she went on about that painting! She thought the colors were too flashy and primitive, the composition was wretched, the people looked like dolls, the painting didn't fit the mood of the room, and the handwriting of the artist's signature was that of a clearly inferior talent.

"*O tempora, o mores,*" she said, staring at the painting with disgust.

She only ever came to my place once of her own accord, and without calling me ahead of time to say she was coming. It was an unfortunate visit. It so happened that my second cousin was visiting with his wife, a surgeon from the Far East.

Emmi D. had a complete command of etiquette and the rules of proper behavior, but she didn't feel it necessary to apply them to anyone not of Caucasian, Christian extraction. I saw how her eyes narrowed as she uttered a greeting and how she insultingly looked past Mei Fang as she withdrew her hand. She then turned to me and said she would come some other time, when I didn't have other guests. Later that evening she called in a very worked up state and wanted to know why I socialize with "jungle people." I lost my temper then, and hung up on her.

Nevertheless, one last time, on a lazy August afternoon, I got the rare impulse to call Emmi D. I asked whether she would like to come over for evening tea. She was silent, perhaps from surprise. Then she asked, "Well, do you still have that painting?"

I knew exactly what painting she meant, of course, but I asked with an air of innocence, "What painting do you mean?"

"The revolutionary painting," she said. "The one over your low bookshelf."

"Oh, that one. It's still there," I said. "Why?"

"In that case," she said, "I'll wait until you replace it with some real art."

After that, I didn't meet her again until my second datura winter, when I saw her standing at the bus stop near the corner of Schaumanninkatu, looking pale, almost yellow, and even more miserable than usual. When I asked her how she was, she admitted to being ill, but wouldn't say what with.

"I'm going in for more tests soon," she said. "*Alea jacta est.* They only have four-person rooms, but I've told them that I won't share a room with anyone of color."

"I hope you get well soon," I said and went on my way, blood boiling. I was sorry that she was unwell, but at that point I really felt that there was no sense in continuing our acquaintance.

And it didn't continue. About a week after our exchange, I met a shared classmate of ours in the tram. She told me that Emmi D. had died.

I examined my feelings. Was I sad, did I have a guilty conscience, or was I perhaps relieved somehow? Everything in me was silent.

"I knew that she was going to the hospital to get tests done," I said. "I saw her just the other week. Who could have thought that she would wither away so quickly?"

"Did you say you met her last week?" my acquaintance asked. "You must be mistaken. She died last month. It was some kind of liver condition. As far as I know she was unconscious for weeks before the end."

"There must be some kind of mix up," I said. "I spoke with her on Schaumanninkatu last Thursday and she was her old self, at least mentally. She's impossible to confuse with anyone else."

"All the same, it must have been someone else," my acquaintance said.

A couple of days later I got a letter from my acquaintance. In it was Emmi's obituary, very austere. Below it were the lines:

Memories are like threads of gold,
They never tarnish or grow old.

Her mother and relatives were listed as the bereaved. She had died the previous month, just as my acquaintance had said.

This incident unnerved me. If the person I had met on Schaumanninkatu was not Emmi D, who was it? If it was Emmi D, or some kind of residual image of her, did other people see her as well, or did they just see me talking to myself on the street corner?

It was time to admit, at least to myself, that my intermittent, and lately chronic, physical and memory problems, had something to do with datura. I had been warned of the consequences, I admit it. I could no longer refuse to connect the increasingly frequent occurrences and unpleasant symptoms I was experiencing to my birthday flower.

I was becoming oversensitive to intense lights, sounds, and smells. I had constant problems with my eyesight. Reading and writing were difficult at times, because I could only see clearly at a very limited distance. My asthma was better, but I was plagued by a constant thirst and even had daily trouble urinating.

After Emmi's death and temporary resurrection, I decided to stop using datura and go back to prescription medication and an inhaler. This resolution was not, however, an easy one to keep.

Faith is Sick

When I think of Faith and Faith's paws, I remember Kachalov's dog, the animal of which Esenin wrote:

> Come, Jim, give me your paw for luck,
> I swear I've never seen one like it.
> Let's go, the two of us, and bark
> Up the moon when Nature's silent.

"Faith is sick," I told the Marquis over the phone. "Come quickly. I think we have to take her to the vet."

Faith had once again been at the office for the day. She lay on the dragon mat and panted. Her nose was dry and hot, her gentle, heavy paws, which I liked to hold in my hands, twitched. She seemed to have fallen into some kind of stupor, but her eyes were open. They didn't react to her immediate surroundings, though. Faith seemed to be looking much further away. She also didn't seem to hear her own name. She was somewhere far away.

I put my hand on her graying warm chest, and my fingertips felt her old heart racing. Your pump is wearing out, I thought. The knowledge was intolerable.

The world was a much better place with old Faith in it than the world would be without her. The dog's death would bring a big change in my life, as well.

Then I had a thought, cruel and frightening. When I left, I had put a handful of datura seeds on a saucer that was on the second lowest

163

shelf of the bookcase. My innocent intention was to buy cactus soil and try to sprout them, just for their beauty. At least that's what I had convinced myself of. I went to look. The stupid fish starting playing and singing, enough to drive a person crazy. I wanted it to be silent forever, so I hit it with the Marquis's ashtray.

There were a few seeds on the saucer, far fewer than I had put there, and they looked damp. Faith could easily reach the second lowest shelf. For some reason she had gone and had a taste of the seeds, probably while I was at the post office. I hadn't even thought that she might take an interest in them. I cursed my own stupidity and carelessness.

When the Marquis came, we lifted the animal, heavy with sickness and age, onto the back seat of the car and covered her with a blanket. She didn't seem to understand or care about what was happening to her.

The Marquis was also miserable. I drove and the Marquis sat in the back. Faith's heavy head rested on his knee and drool dripped onto his pants, but he didn't care. On the way, I told him about the datura seeds in a rushed and confused manner. He didn't have a single word of reproach, but that only made me feel all the worse.

The veterinarian's waiting room was crowded, and we were forced to wait. I was afraid Faith would die in our arms. The pauses between her labored breaths grew longer. The dog's breathing had become a measure of time.

As the young vet listened to Faith's heart, I asked whether she had ever heard of datura and did she know what antidotes to use for its toxins. She shook her head—she'd never even heard the plant's name.

"Of course, you can always call the Poison Information Center," I said, "but this is urgent. Give her an antidote for scopolamine and hyoscyamine and nicotine. You must have something suitable."

"Stomach pump first," she said.

"Do you think she'll make it?" I asked after the procedure. Faith looked nearly lifeless.

"It's impossible to say," she said. "Her heart is quite weak, as you know. We'll just have to wait and see. She'll have to stay here overnight for observation. This kind of thing is always touch and go with such an old animal."

We left in low spirits, without saying much of anything to one another. I think the Marquis was also thinking that we had seen Faith alive for the last time.

The Psychology of a Plant

I called the Ethnobotanist and asked if I could meet him somewhere.

"Do you want me to write another article?" he asked.

"Actually I need some information on a plant. Or, rather, I need to talk to you about it. I already know quite a bit about it myself."

"Is it urgent?"

"I'd say so."

"What plant?"

"Devil's trumpet—datura."

"Alright, I'll come over," he promised.

At the office, with a fresh cup of coffee in front of him, he skipped the small talk and got straight down to business.

"A very interesting plant, in its own way. As you probably already know, it's a member of the nightshade family, along with potato and tomato plants, tobacco and henbane. In tropical countries and temperate zones, it can spread like a weed. Beautiful, but to be avoided. I haven't acquainted myself too closely with it, and I don't intend to. Maybe you have?"

"Yes, I have."

"I actually find datura a bit distasteful. Its blossoms are too grand and ostentatious if you ask me. For a herbaceous plant, it's huge. You probably already know that it's also poisonous, which is to say it has an extraordinarily well developed defense mechanism. A plant like that is full of energy and aggression. Did you know that it's considered an evil goddess by some?"

"Why?"

"It's said that the plant has a criminal past, though datura itself can hardly be blamed for that. In the Middle Ages, particularly in Italy, poisoners used it for assassinations. Datura contains a number of poisons. It also contains Vitamin C, but it's probably wiser to get that from oranges or vitamin pills. The main alkaloid in datura seeds is hyoscyamine, the same substance found in henbane. The seeds also contain scopolamine and atropine, which have been used as arrow poison and eye medicine. The leaves of the plant contain methanol and hyoscine. The stem contains nicotine and pyridine, umbelliferone and tannin and a couple of dozen other toxins. It does have its medicinal uses, though, as do all poisons. It has been grown in secret gardens and used for religious and therapeutic purposes, such as to treat wounds and internal damage. It dries the mucous membranes. Did you know that…"

"…it has even been used to try to cure asthma," I said.

"Exactly. Its effects are unpredictable, however. It numbs the senses. Don't keep it in your bedroom at night."

"Are you serious?" I asked with mock lightness. "Will it come after me and throttle me in my sleep? It's only a pretty flower."

"Only! As I recall, we've talked before about how plants and their mentalities are underestimated. As a thinking woman, you shouldn't fall into that trap. I mean it. Datura smells the strongest at night. Its scent alone can give you hallucinations. Datura breaks down the wall between fantasy and reality, making it impossible to tell them apart. I repeat: impossible! The boundary becomes invisible. You could slip onto the wrong side, so to say, completely unawares. If that happens, there'll be the devil to pay."

Then I confessed to him that, from time to time, once or twice a week, I drank tea made from datura leaves for my asthma, or crushed a couple of seeds into powder and then sprinkled them on a sandwich.

"Kind of like a condiment," I said with a forced laugh. "But I've stopped using it, really."

("Really" meaning that I still, on some nights, out of habit, put a datura leaf in my tea strainer, just one, and mixed the drink with ordinary tea.)

The Ethnobotanist didn't laugh.

"Unwise," he said sharply. "Very, very unwise. I wouldn't have thought you'd stray into something like that. You're a grown woman for heaven's sake! I'm warning you! The datura's toxins accumulate in the body. Your vital organs will begin start to shut down. You'll begin forgetting things. You might even forget to take your next breath. The seeds and root in particular are pure poison. Eating more than just a few seeds is certain death, and the concentration of poison in them can vary wildly. Eating them could lead to undocumented, long-term consequences. But it's the root that is the most dangerous. Keep away from it!"

I began to sweat, but he went on with his merciless lecture. "Do you want to lose your awareness of time and place? Do you want to lose your memory? Suffer from mental breakdowns, perhaps chronically?"

"Of course not."

"Tell me, have you already had...experiences?"

I hesitated.

"I suppose you could say so," I confessed.

He waited for me to give him more details, but I remained silent.

"Can you be more specific? Have you suffered from nausea? Dizziness? A dry mouth and thirst?"

"You'd think you're a doctor, not a botanist."

"Have you?"

He waited, unsmiling, for my answer.

"Well, from time to time."

"I knew it," he said. "Dilated pupils? Lost time? Confusion of time and place? Oversensitivity to light and sound? Palpitations? Overly vivid dreams? Communication with people who aren't physically there?"

I remembered my run-in with Emmi D, who was dead, getting lost, my states of agitation and anxiety, my eyesight problems, some conversations that weren't conversations at all, and I swallowed.

"I knew it," he said again, unhappy. "No one can use datura without consequences. You've gotten off easy, seeing as you can still carry on a conversation with me. Some people get lost completely in other realities and never return to our shared world. You could have died.

Promise me—don't even look at that flower again. Give it away, or better yet, destroy it. It has too much power over you already.

He was right. But I still didn't want to destroy my beautiful flower.

The Woman Who Was Four

When someone dies in a movie or on stage, the face of the actor—
even smeared with fake blood—doesn't really differ from the faces of
the living. Real death, however, shrinks the face and alters the features.
In half an hour, they have become nearly unrecognizable. Their owner
seems to have abandoned them, and those left behind by the deathbed
cannot help but ask, "Where has she gone?"

All cadavers resemble one another. All that was personal and
characteristic in the face is stripped away. It is only then that one
understands that it is not so much a person's features that shape their
face, but rather it is the person's experiences and memories that give
the face its unique, familiar, and beloved appearance. And those
elements the departed take with them when they go.

It was Sylvia, the woman who was four, who led me to these
thoughts. No doubt in part because I talked with the woman, if I
remember correctly, in the same week I heard about Emmi's death. I
never discovered whether Sylvia was faking it, sick, crazy, eccentric, or
"the real thing."

I suppose she could also be considered one of the Otherkin. Sylvia
was middle-aged and formerly employed in middle management. She
had been laid off in the recession, gotten divorced, and then fell deeply
into debt. If one were to indulge in a bit of amateur psychology, one
might suggest that those experiences played a part in her peculiar
situation.

"I am not just one," Sylvia said. "I am a group of people with only

one body. You're about to ask who live in me. You know my name.
I, the one speaking now, have always lived in this body. But I'm also
home to an older gentleman, a girl I call Fanni, and a horrible brat of
a boy, a real nuisance. Sometimes I think there are still more people in
me, but they stay so quiet that I haven't noticed them."

I remember Saulus saying that people have seven bodies. And now
someone was claiming that one body could hold many identities!

"How long have they lived in you?" I asked, incredulous.

"One of them has been there since the start, since childhood. The
other two moved in later."

She talked about herself like she was a house!

"Would it be possible for me to meet these people?" I asked, curious
and disbelieving at the same time. I found the thought fascinating
that this person could hold all four seasons, four periods of life.

"Why not—maybe soon if you're interested. Oh, look, it's raining,"
Sylvia said, got out of the armchair, and went to the window. "I have
to go. Goodbye."

But she made no move to leave. She stayed where she stood, silent,
before letting out a heavy sigh. I could only see her neck and back,
which now seemed hunched. Water trickled hurriedly down the
window pane, each drop forking into two or three branches. The
stark view outside the window dimmed, the brick wall and dark sky
becoming one. The lamp on my desk seemed to lose its intensity, and
the woman's silhouette seemed to dissolve into the gloom.

"It's just a shower."

I was startled to hear a deep baritone reverberate in the room. I
hadn't heard anyone come in, and no one had. He had been there
the whole time, I just hadn't realized it. Sylvia turned away from the
window, and I saw her face again, except that it was not hers, not
Sylvia's.

"Sylvia left," a man said. "I'm Antero."

Features that had a moment ago looked like the flourishing face of
a woman in her prime had become lined and masculine. Her body
language had changed entirely. I saw a bent figure, an old man, though
one dressed in women's clothing. I couldn't get a word out.

"You're shocked, afraid even," he said. "I apologize, you must not be used to this sort of thing."

"You could say that," I admitted in a shaky voice. "Would you like to sit down?"

I was trying to be polite, though I hoped that this person wouldn't stay long.

"Thank you," he said, and sat in the same armchair that Sylvia had just gotten up from. "I won't keep you," he went on, as if having guessed my thoughts. "But I could say a thing or two to help you get over your shock. This is natural, completely natural!"

I wasn't convinced by this claim, it sounded utterly ridiculous.

"The body, if I may be so bold, is a gate, a road wide enough for more than one traveler. In fact, I think that folks are naturally multiple, a family of selves, but our upbringing and schooling trim us down like you'd do to the branches of a tree."

"Well! That's a new theory to me."

"Society tries to fix us as one, always the same. But that's a big lie, and it won't work even if you try. If you really looked at yourself, you'd know there's more than one of you as well. You've got both sexes and all ages in you. The person you think you are is just a small part of all your selves. Most folks just don't want to admit it."

I found the idea objectionable. I admit that I remember many times when I "wasn't myself," as one says. But usually those times had to do with shame or guilt. It takes courage to admit that the person who had acted in those situations was me and no one else.

"I think one has to seek to be whole," I said. "At times I feel like I'm not the one who did what I did, or at least that it wasn't at all typical of me. And you often hear people who regret what they've done say, 'I wasn't myself,' but that's different. It doesn't mean people have distinct selves."

"Don't be so sure. Think about it," the man said. "This is a fascinating subject, but I can't stay. Maybe I'll stop by again for another chat. You have another meeting now."

"Do I?" I said. "I don't think so."

"She's already here," Antero said. "You have a nice day."

His old voice faded as the being in front of me grew young and lithe.

"What's that?" asked the girl who was wearing Sylvia's clothes.

She pointed at the rock 'n' roll fish and went to have a closer look. The fish began mewling in its synthetic voice, and the girl laughed with surprise. She danced around a little and then seemed to get embarrassed.

"Are you Fanni?" I asked and went to silence the fish.

"I guess so," the girl said, a little unsure. "You wanted to meet me? Why?"

"Just out of curiosity," I said. "How long have you been…or, rather, lived…"

"In Sylvia? A couple of years," the girl said, as if talking about a rental apartment. She was about to say something else, but before she could, her face twisted and some kind of spasm shook her whole body. I watched this new metamorphosis in shock. She stomped her foot and was no longer Fanni. It had been a very short visit.

"What do you think of my acquaintances?" Sylvia asked. "Fanni didn't want to go."

I was bewildered by the blur of events and the sudden switches of people, or at least characters.

"I haven't met all of them yet," I managed to say.

"Thank goodness for that. You really don't want to meet the fourth one. An ill-mannered child, a real menace. One day I'll find a way to evict him."

"When you leave and they take your place, where do you go?"

"Sometimes I just go out like a candle and I'm completely gone. That can happen even if I resist. But sometimes I'm in control and can observe the situation and intervene like I did just now driving Fanni away."

"Can I be frank about what I think of your acquaintances?"

"Go ahead."

"I'm not completely convinced. Despite everything, I have trouble believing that all these people I've met are different from you, separate individuals."

"So you think I'm acting for you? Faking it?"

I tried to be considerate. "That's not really what I meant. Perhaps it's some kind of compulsion, unconscious."

"Don't give me that tired old garbage. I've been to six different therapists," she snapped, so angry that I regretted having said anything. "Dissociative hysteria. Ha! I was just thirteen when my parents took me to the first. That one suspected my poor father of incest, that gentle and warm man who conscientiously paid his ridiculous fees."

"That must have been difficult," I said in an effort to sound compassionate. In fact, I was still terrified and afraid her face would change again.

To my relief, Sylvia took her coat from the hanger and made to leave. Just her? They all were leaving in the same plaid coat.

"I don't think we have anything left to talk about," she said coldly and turned on her heel.

When the door had slammed shut, someone tapped on the window, and I heard giggling and light footsteps running. I thought that Penjami had come by, and I climbed up on a stool to see out. Some menace had drawn a bad word in the dust on the window and run off. Whoever it was, they were probably dressed in Sylvia's coat.

A PECULIAR FLOWER SHOP

Even when the streets are slippery with ice, summer fields are always with me. Florists' windows are the joys of my evening walks. I can't resist stopping at each floral window, and never a week goes by in mid-winter that I don't come up with a reason to visit a flower shop.

There are florists whose window arrangements seem to radiate out into the street. Other windows are like caves whose depths are illuminated by blossoms. Like campfires, they warm the people wandering the wintery streets. Each flower, though a captive, is an entire summer in miniature. I could stand by a window like that all evening.

When I open the door of a flower shop, my breathing deepens and slows. The room is saturated by a seductive aroma, and my eyes answer the calls of cloaked nectar, though the calls are not meant for me. The hieroglyphs that nature paints on the blossoms are signposts to insects looking for food. They are promises of coming pleasure and of the flower's resurrection, the birth of another new summer.

The world's beauty, so cruel and incredible, always has a purpose. It's never there for entertainment. It is a fighting beauty, always a necessity. How can it also be such a feast for our senses?

That day, I had intended to buy a poinsettia. Maybe I would take it to my aunt, maybe I'd keep it myself, I hadn't decided.

The flower shop was crowded with people buying Christmas baskets decorated with silk bows, spiral candles, and lichen. Plastic elves had been shoved between hyacinths, lilies of the valley, and red tulips.

The arrangements were tasteless and the flowers looked a bit wilted. I couldn't see the usual saleswoman, the people behind the counter complete strangers. I supposed the shop had changed owners.

"Where's the other lady?" asked a woman in a black dress who was holding a potted white azalea. She didn't seem happy either.

"Oh, she switched careers," said one of the new salespersons, a short blonde woman whose hair hung down past her shoulders. She didn't look at the woman who had asked the question. The older of the two women was tying a bouquet of lilies with hurried motions. I guessed they were mother and daughter. The atmosphere in the shop was agitated and unpleasant, but that was to be expected at Christmas time.

Just as my turn came up, I happened to look up at the top shelf, which was stacked with pots and vases, and saw a pretty little basket woven from birch bark. I was overcome by an intense desire to buy it. I decided I would plant my poinsettia in it.

"How much is that?" I asked.

"I can't remember the price, but I'll check it for you," the younger woman said in a bored voice. I was embarrassed to have troubled her at this busy time. She climbed up a step ladder to reach the bark basket. On the way down she slipped and nearly lost her balance.

"Look out! Don't step on those," the older woman said and pointed at something on the floor behind the counter that I couldn't see.

"Of course I won't," the blond woman snapped. "Don't order me around!"

The unexpected severity of her reaction surprised me. Maybe she had just had a bad fright from her slip. It was strange to see her face darken with rage from such a harmless little comment. Her pretty mouth twisted into a malevolent expression. She bared her teeth like a mongrel dog.

I had a bill ready in my hand. Instead of calming down and taking my money, this strange person ignored me completely and just stared angrily at her colleague, who was perhaps also her mother. Not necessarily the happiest of arrangements, I thought.

The awkward moment just wouldn't pass. The daughter's voice grew louder and higher. She was speaking very quickly now, scolding and cursing, but I couldn't make out the words. It sounded like she had switched to some unknown tongue.

The older woman didn't turn or answer. She was still trying to finish the bouquet, but I could see her hands trembling and her forehead turning red. All of a sudden, the worked up saleswoman jumped behind her mother and hit her hard between the shoulder blades. Then the victim lost her patience, she grunted, turned, and quick as lightning, slapped her assaulter across the cheek. The daughter spat in her mother's face.

The azalea lady in the black dress looked shocked.

"What are you doing?" she yelled. "At Christmas of all times!"

The women didn't seem to hear her. They were fighting silently now except for groaning and panting, as if they were in some kind of wrestling match. Without my noticing, they had moved from behind the counter to the middle of the floor, maybe to get more room for their scuffle, which was intensifying. The other customers drew into a tighter and tighter circle. They didn't say anything, didn't try to stop what was going on, not even the old azalea lady. Just the opposite, everyone was watching the incident, wide eyed, as if it were a professional bout they had paid to see. I was afraid I'd soon hear applause and cheering, but the audience's silence remained unbroken.

Most terrifying of all, it seemed like the flowers had turned towards the sudden flash of violence as if mesmerized. Were the buds swelling and the blossoms becoming more exuberant? Were the colors deepening as if a bright light had been shined on them?

The women's heels clattered on the floor as they tried to kick each other. In the heat of their battle, a glass vase filled with flowers was knocked off the window sill and shattered. The women trampled the flowers under their heels. Petals were strewn everywhere like drops of blood. I was overtaken by fear and panic.

I pushed my way to the door. The crowd gave way slowly and unwillingly. The unusual duel seemed to have captured its full attention. I escaped the store empty handed just as the grunting and clattering of heels was joined by yells and cries. Part of the shop window crashed onto the sidewalk.

When I got home, I realized I had left a plastic bag in the store.

Though it only held a couple of oranges and the daily paper, I was still annoyed.

When Noora called that evening, I mentioned that the flower shop had changed owners and that the new ladies seemed a bit strange. For some reason, I didn't want to tell even her what had actually happened. What had actually happened? Did I even know that myself?

"I don't think the store has changed owners," Noora said.

After the holidays, about a week later, I passed by the same store. As I was fleeing, I had heard the sound of glass shattering, but the window was undamaged now. They must have replaced the glass. There was no sign of the incident. The flower arrangements were particularly beautiful that day: blue hydrangeas, poinsettias, simple and elegant baskets of hyacinths.

Christmas was over, but I still wanted a poinsettia, and I remembered that I needed to buy a bottle of seaweed extract. I wasn't eager to see the arguing women again, but my longing for flowers overcame my hesitation, and I ventured into the store. Besides, I hoped to find the plastic bag with my oranges and out-of-date daily paper. To my relief, the former owner was inside tying a mourning band around a wreath.

"Oh, you're back," I said.

"Back?" she said. "But I haven't been gone."

"And the window has been fixed," I said before I fully understood what she had said.

"It was never broken," the woman said, even more confused. "Not in my time, at least. And I've been here for a long time, almost twelve years now. You must be thinking of a different shop."

I was embarrassed and said, "I'm sure you're right—it must have been a different flower shop."

But when I looked up at the top shelf, I saw the small birch bark basket that I had wanted to buy. I knew that I was in the same shop where the brawl had happened. It was the same to me, at least, but perhaps not to everyone else.

I didn't want the basket anymore, and I didn't dare ask whether anyone had forgotten a plastic bag full of oranges in the flower shop. My life had become stranger than the articles in *The New Anomalist*.

The Fastest Way to Travel

Faith had recovered, though very slowly. Her heart medication had been increased, and the prognosis was that she only had a short time left. The Marquis never left her alone in his apartment, and now always brought her to the office during the day, though only on the condition that there were no datura seeds anywhere. I assured him that I wouldn't think of keeping them in the office anymore.

Faith spent her diminishing days asleep on the dragon mat, and I had to half carry her to do her business in the empty lot next to the railway tracks.

Raikka had also come back after a short break. He finally brought his article on hole teleportation. Neither of us mentioned his finger, but I could see that the end of it was still wrapped in bandages. I suspected it hadn't healed properly.

"Hole teleportation is the fastest and best way to travel," Raikka assured me.

I wished that Raikka hadn't come just that day. I was having one of my bad moments, and it was hard to focus my eyes, let alone get excited about hole teleportation. My head was humming. I had drunk at least a gallon of water. I decided, once again, that I would have to give up datura tea, completely. As soon as he came in, Raikka said, "It smells funny in here."

"Could you tell me, in a couple of words, what hole teleportation is," I asked. "I don't have the time right now to read your article." (In fact, I wasn't able to.)

"Hole teleportation uses the geometric characteristics of the universe to move objects. It sounds amazing, but any object or creature can be transported to any point in the universe just as long as it's first shifted outside the universe."

"Really?" I said. "And just how does one go about that?"

"You see, if you send an object outside the universe, where there is no time or space, the object can't stay there, of course. That's why it instantaneously appears at a different point in our universe. Before the object is sent out, it's enclosed in a vacuum made of virtual holes. It's now completely isolated and in a place that is not a place, in a time that is not time, a location governed by the geometry of a black hole."

"Is that so?"

I was very dull-witted that day. As far as I could see, I still hadn't gotten an answer to how the object is enclosed in a virtual hole in order to zap it somewhere inside the universe, but I couldn't bring myself to ask.

"An object in a virtual vacuum is stored perfectly. Nowhere could be safer. Take a small atomic bomb, say on the scale of Hiroshima, or even a bigger one, maybe five thousand megatons, and detonate it next to an object in a virtual vacuum. What happens?"

"You tell me."

"Nothing at all! And imagine how cheap it would be to send spaceships deep into space, into other galaxies. No fuel costs!"

"Imagine!" I repeated out of politeness.

"Speaking of transportation, did you notice that there was an interesting test on the beltway a while ago? They tested an autopilot system."

"On the beltway? Was it last spring?" He had my attention now.

"I think so. They closed it from traffic for a couple of hours in the early morning. A dozen or so cars drove several miles without drivers, just using on-board computers. Really advanced technology! Soon no one will need driver's licenses!"

This piece of news cheered me up considerably. I hadn't told anyone about the phantom convoy, because I had convinced myself I was seeing things. I had tried to forget what I had seen, just like many other chaotic and dreamlike events that year.

Raikka had already moved on to another subject. He promised to write an article about how to extract energy from a vacuum for our next issue, and one on the relationship between consciousness and random systems for the issue after that, and for the June special issue...

I stopped listening to his promises. I couldn't help thinking about the vision that was actually real. It proved to me that the city itself had begun to resemble a giant hallucination, and that it was getting harder and harder to tell private and shared delusions apart.

A Visitation

One cold night, when I got home from a long day at the office, a strange woman, dressed in white, was waiting for me in my bedroom. I wasn't frightened, just surprised. I couldn't tell whether the woman was young or old, ugly or beautiful. She was sitting in front of the window on the stool that I had inherited from the kitchen of my childhood home. The darkening sky was behind her. Because the evening light streamed into the room from behind the stranger, I couldn't make out her features. My datura plant had long bloomed and flourished on that same stool, until the day I took it out to the summer house and abandoned it to the night frost. However, I still had a jam jar full of dried datura leaves on the top shelf of the kitchen cupboard. Its lid was shut tight, and I should have wondered why the whole room seemed filled with the smell of datura that evening.

"Who are you," I asked, "and how did you get inside?"

"That's not important," she said.

"Oh yes it is," I said. "I didn't invite you, and I want you to leave."

Paying no attention to my command, she said, "Have you ever thought that someone who has never seen cannot know what blindness is. And if everyone else is blind, they'd never know they'd missed anything. The same is true for all the senses, of course. We could draw far-ranging conclusions from this fact, but do we have the courage to?"

"It's late," I said. "I don't have the energy for philosophical discussions. I'm going to bed."

And as if it were completely normal that, in my bedroom, sitting on the stool I had inherited from my parents, was an uninvited woman in a white dress giving a lecture, I got ready for bed. I undressed, brushed my teeth, washed, put on my nightgown, fluffed up my pillow, and drew the blanket up around my neck. All the while, the woman in the white dress droned on. I didn't feel particularly unbalanced at the time, which I now find very strange.

"Do we ever mourn," the woman went on, "that we lack a lateral line system, or that we aren't able to find our way as well as migratory birds or that we can't use seismic waves like elephants? No, we don't feel like we're missing anything, we don't desire more sense or more senses. And yet, other species have numerous senses that would reveal reality to us in an entirely different light. Not only that, but many of the senses we share are much more acute in them. That means they have information that we lack. It means we can't even imagine what the world would be like if we had senses that we lack. It means that we don't understand reality nearly as well as we think. No, we don't understand it at all."

"Actually, can you imagine," I said, turning onto my side to face the visitor, "That I know all about that. I've been thinking a lot about those sort of things. You speak as if with my voice, but I still just don't have the energy to listen to you…"

During those years, it seemed like everywhere I went everyone was lecturing me, wanting to teach me, even preach to me, as if I was still a schoolchild, one in need of remedial education even. But this woman was saying aloud what I had been thinking to myself.

"You've learned to look around you in a certain way, you've been told what to see, and that's what you see," she went on. "You have been taught to hear and react to certain sounds. Others you avoid hearing. Don't be afraid. If you want to, you can see and hear differently, more accurately, more perfectly."

Half asleep, I heard, "Haven't you ever thought that all those people who experience hallucinations, something that other people don't experience, have actually discovered a new sense or at least that their existing senses have become more sensitive? I know you are one of those people. Embrace the change! Seek out new alternatives! There's no reason to assume that so-called delusions are mistaken observations, false interpretations of reality. At times, they provide information that would be impossible to receive with normal senses. Hallucinations could be observations that we normally ignore, because they disrupt our received understanding of reality."

"Exactly," I nodded. "That's just what I've been thinking."

"The flower you saw as a child…"

"You mean…. How do you know about that flower, the crown imperial?"

"That doesn't matter. Trust your eyes! Heed the testimony of your senses! What you experience is always true. This is important. This is a fundamental truth."

She was gone. I wasn't surprised by that either. I just fell asleep in my bed, which had become a merry-go-round.

"THUS UNENLIGHTENED,
LOST IN ERROR'S MAZE"

"What on earth are you doing?" someone asked. Was it the person who I always felt was sitting in the back seat, even when I knew I was driving alone?

"What do you mean what am I doing?" I answered. "Can't you see I'm driving. It's an emergency. Don't distract me."

I had never driven so fast. I was terribly frightened, but I knew that I couldn't stop. I wasn't sure where I was going or why, but I knew I had to drive, to keep the car on the road even at that speed. The road must have been surfaced with quiet asphalt, so silent was the car as it sped on.

"You're not in a car. We're at the office. You're sitting in the armchair and you're sick," the Marquis said. "I'll call an ambulance."

"Don't, they make so much noise, no ambulances, and I'm already driving myself anyway."

Now I understood why I was in such a hurry.

You know what happened after that. I was in treatment for months. Malignant changes were found in my blood, my heart had been damaged, my fatigue was chronic. But the worst was the fear that took hold of me as I began to understand that I was losing my grip on the shared world. I couldn't be sure whether the conversations I had were real conversations or just projections of my own thoughts.

I couldn't be certain that the people I met were flesh and blood. My memory, the anchor that bound me to shared perceptions, had come loose. I was adrift.

Was it you who, when things were at their worst at the beginning, visited me and read to me aloud. It helped. Was it you who read this verse:

"Thus on a stormy sea my bark is borne
By adverse winds, and with rough tempest tost;
Thus unenlightened, lost in error's maze,
My blind opinion, ever dubious strays."

The truth is always shared. A reality that belongs to only one person isn't real.

As my sick leave continued and my recovery dragged on, the Marquis was sorry to have to tell me that we could no longer continue working together. I agreed. I didn't even want to think about *The New Anomalist*.

I was put on a disability pension, and for over ten years now, sanatorium visits and outpatient treatment have given my life its rhythm. Many times, I found myself in the line where I once thought I saw my old schoolmate, Viveca.

I haven't kept in touch with the Marquis at all, but I've heard that *The New Anomalist* is still coming out. To my surprise, I've found that I miss many of the magazine's contributors, young Raikka, Saulus, Mr. Chance, even Loogaroo.

I spend more time in the city than before. I sit in the parks or in market cafés, I wander through libraries and bookshops, galleries, sales, open lectures, flea markets, taste tests, and product demonstrations. In the evenings, I go to cultural events that are free or nearly free. It does no good to be holed up inside four walls.

My hair has thinned and lost its color. Whenever I can spare the money, I go to the hairdresser to give it a bit of volume, and also because I enjoy talking with the Hair Artiste. Yes, her, the angel boy's mother, who wrote her doctoral dissertation on the hairdos of the independence day ball. She still receives some clients at her home.

She meticulously curls my thin hair, and sometimes refuses to take my money.

Though I stopped using datura ages ago, though I bid farewell to my flower, the woman in the white dress still visits some evenings and sits in the corner of my room. She hasn't grown any older, though I still can't see her face, as she always sits with the light behind her, and when I turn on the lamp, she has already turned her back to me. Her breath smells of datura, but its stink now makes me shudder.

Often she just sits there without saying a word, but sometime she opens her mouth and continues her lessons.

"I'm not listening to you," I say. "You're a temptress, an evil goddess."

Then I head into the city or take a bath, read, call my sister, turn on the television, and make a cup of tea—real tea.

Sometimes the woman vanishes instantly. Sometimes dawn will break before she goes, taking the stink of datura with her.

WITH A FINGER TO HIS LIPS

I had agreed to an early meeting at the library café, and I took a shortcut through Dufva park. I was early, as I often am these days, and the weather was wonderful, so I decided to sit for a moment on a sunny park bench on which someone had abandoned a free paper. I started leafing through it to pass the time. The city's main eastern artery was just a couple of hundred yards away, and the morning rush hour was just getting started. The elated song of starlings and chaffinches mingled with the ceaseless rumble of traffic.

I was reading an article about a government cloud-seeding experiment that had led to the deaths of hundreds of people, and I thought that even the most paranoid of *The New Anomalist*'s readers wouldn't have thought to suspect anything of the sort. Suddenly I heard a swish. Startled, I looked up. The shadows of the trees moved back and forth on the gravel of the park path as before. A girl sped past me on a scooter, hair streaming in the wind. On another park path, a mother bent over to tie a different child's shoe laces. A hot air balloon was sailing past the fresh gold leaf of the cathedral's dome, and, above it, a jet left a foamy contrail.

But something had changed. It took me a moment to realize what was going on. A great silence had descended. The familiar landscape of sound had been wiped away. The scooter turned and the girl rushed past my bench in the other direction, but the wheels made no sound as they rolled on the gravelly path. The jet flew over the city in silence. It was as if all the most everyday sounds had been sucked out of the city and sealed in an invisible container.

Everything began to seem like a silent movie. I got up, uneasy, and put the paper in the garbage can next to the bench without it causing the least rustle. I looked past a row of budding trees to the street, where people were hurrying to work, school, and the stores. The traffic lights turned green, and the unbroken lines of cars jerked forward, but my ears couldn't make out a thing—no sounds of tires, motors, or footsteps.

It was oppressive. I shook my head, lifted my hands to my ears and patted them. Had something happened to both my ears? Was it possible to suddenly just go deaf?

A movement made me look back. On the bench that I had just left now sat a man in a grey suit with an old backpack in his lap. Where had he come from all of sudden? There was something familiar about him. He raised his hand in greeting to someone and nodded to me. Or was it me he was greeting? I looked around, but as there was no one else nearby, I nodded back, though uncertainly and nearly imperceptibly. Because of my nearsightedness I didn't recognize him right away.

I hesitated before approaching the bench. The man rose, lifted a finger, and motioned for me to follow him. Now I recognized him: the Master of Sound, the mumbling man, as gray as ever. I found I was happy to see him after so many years.

The Master of Sound walked purposefully ahead of me, carrying his backpack, and I followed, unquestioning, as if in a dream. There is a round glass-roofed stage in the park for bands to play on. The view from there took in the park, the market square, the boulevard, even the harbor. The Master of Sound climbed the short steps onto the stage, put down his backpack, and turned to face me. He spoke to me from the stage, or maybe he whispered, but I couldn't hear a word, not even mumbling. I pointed to my ear and said, quite loudly I think, "I can't hear a thing."

And I couldn't, not even my own voice. That made me unhappy.

The Master of Sound put a finger to his lips and flashed a mysterious smile. He gestured for me to come closer. He seemed to have something to show me. He began rummaging through his backpack.

His mouth opened again. I followed the movement of his lips, and I thought I could read the words: "Here it is!"

The Master of Sound lifted up a canister, similar to the one he had shown me at the office, though much larger. I understood that it was the new model of the Sound Swallower that he had promised to come show me long ago. Now it was finished. Now it worked. You didn't even have to lift it to your ear—it worked from a distance. The Sound Swallower had devoured the clamor of the city. Maybe all its residents were now living in the same silence.

My face must have reflected disbelief and confusion. With graceful gestures, the Master of Sound led me to understand that he had something else in his backpack to show me. He plunged his hand into the bag again and brought out a long object wrapped in tissue paper.

"Is it a new device?" I tried to ask.

Maybe the Master of Sound heard my question or read it on my lips, because he nodded. He slowly formed a new word on his lips. I thought I saw him say: "Im-age Swal-low-er."

But when he had opened the package, I was confused. It wasn't a device at all, it was a flower.

He was holding my flower, the first one, the one I knew was unknown. I was certain that it wasn't just the same species, but exactly the same specimen. It glowed with the same light as back then, every panther spot was in place, every speck of pollen where they were once before. How had he gotten a hold of the flower across a distance of so many years? How had it stayed fresh after all this time?

I tried to ask him, but he put a finger to his lips again. Then he made a gesture that encompassed the entire view before us and pointed at the flower of my childhood. He lifted it to my eyes so all I could see was the flower's deep blossom.

What light came streaming from the flower! It filled my eyes, my head, spread throughout the park like a radiant cloud eradicating all shadows and outlines, even the flower's own colors. It absorbed the trees, the streams of cars and people, the apartment buildings, department stores, factories and cathedrals, even the sea and the spring. Nothing was spared.

Now I was deaf and blind, but someone touched my hand in the milky silence, and led me forward, perhaps down the same steps I had ascended to the stage. Though I had lost my most important senses, I wasn't sorry or afraid. I felt that whoever was leading me wasn't the Master of Sound, but the flower itself. Its leaf rested in my hand like another hand and took me towards the ultimate secret of existence, and I was willing to trade all that had come before in exchange for it.

This state was pierced by a scream that made my ears pop open again. A girl's crying restored the lost city. Its sounds rushed back, and once again I heard life's counterpoint. The fog cleared around me. The girl was the same as the one who had sped up and down the path on a scooter just a moment ago. She had fallen right in front of me and hurt her knee on the gravel. A thin trickle of blood ran down her tanned shin.

I meant to help the sobbing girl up and ask, "Are you alright?" I wanted to, but I hesitated and missed my chance. She had already stopped crying with a short hiccup, gotten back up on her scooter, and soldiered bravely on. I wasn't needed.

I looked around, trying to find the hand that had led me and the Master of Sound. I wanted an explanation, I wanted the flower for myself, but it was too late. The Master of Sound had taken it with him.

ABOUT THE AUTHOR:

Leena Krohn is one of the most respected Finnish writers of her generation. She was awarded the prestigious Finlandia Prize for best novel for *Matemaattisia olioita tai jaettuja unia (Mathematical Beings)*. Her short novel *Tainaron: Mail From Another City*, first published in English in 2004, was nominated for a World Fantasy Award. Most recently, Krohn won the Aleksis Kivi Fund Award from the Finnish Literature Society, for lifetime achievement and a "commitment to high-quality, ethically uncompromising fiction."

ABOUT THE TRANSLATORS:

Anna Volmari is a Finnish, internationally educated freelance translator. J. Robert Tupasela is a Finnish-Australian, New-York-raised translator. Between them they have two decades of translation experience and have lived in five countries on three continents. They collaborate on literary translations between Finnish and English, including English translations of Finnish authors Leena Krohn, Jyrki Vainonen and Carita Forsgren and Finnish translations of two crime novels by James Thompson. They live in Helsinki with two cats and a mountain of books.

OTHER BOOKS AVAILABLE
FROM CHEEKY FRAWG

Cheeky Frawg has made a strong commitment to Nordic/Scandinavian fiction, reflected in our current offerings…

Print and E-book

Jagannath by Karin Tidbeck. Enter the strange and wonderful world of Swedish sensation Karin Tidbeck with this feast of darkly fantastical short stories. Whether through the falsified historical record of the uniquely weird Swedish creature known as the "Pyret" or the title story, "Jagannath," about a biological ark in the far future, Tidbeck's unique imagination will enthrall, amuse, and unsettle you. How else to describe a collection that includes "Cloudberry Jam," a story that opens with the line "I made you in a tin can"? Winner of the Crawford Award and shortlisted for the World Fantasy Award. Introduction by Elizabeth Hand.

The Explorer & Other Stories by Jyrki Vainonen.) This sly book showcases the quietly strange, unsettling short fiction of this acclaimed Finnish writer. Vainonen is renowned for his Finnish translations of the works of Seamus Heaney, Jonathan Swift and William Shakespeare. Vainonen's first collection of short stories was awarded the Helsingin Sanomat Literature Prize and his work has been featured in such iconic collections as the *Dedalus Book of Finnish Fantasy*. This first English-language collection includes stories from Jyrki Vainonen's three collections and is translated by J. Robert Tupasela and Anna Volmari, with one story translated by Hilde Hawkins. "Vainonen's deceptively cool voice lured me into a world where horrors and wonders lurk just beneath the surface." – Karin Tidbeck, *Jagannath*

E-book only

It Came from the North edited by Desirina Boskovich. This anthology of Finnish fantasy features fiction from Jyrki Vainonen, Leena Krohn, Johanna Sinisalo, Hannu Rajaniemi, Anne Leinonen, Tiina Raevaara and many more—including Pasi Ilmari Jaaskelainen, author of the critically acclaimed *The Rabbit Back Literature Society*. What will you find within these pages? A photographer stumbles on a wounded troll, and attempts to nurse it back to health. A lonely girl discovers the flames in the family smithy are tied to an ancient portal between worlds. A peculiar swamp holds restorative powers, for its avian and human inhabitants alike. *It Came From the North* offers a diverse selection of fifteen fantastical tales including stories from some of Finland's most respected writers, alongside up-and-coming talents who are redefining the rules of contemporary literature.

Tainaron by Leena Krohn. The classic novel by an iconic Finnish author, a finalist for the World Fantasy Award. Tainaron: a city like no other, populated by talking insects, as observed by the nameless narrator, who is far from home. A World Fantasy Award finalist. Afterword by Matthew Cheney. "The novel contains scenes of startling beauty and strangeness that change how the reader sees the world. Krohn effortlessly melds the literal with the metaphorical, so that the narrator's exploration of the city through its inhabitants encompasses both the speculation of science fiction and the resonant symbolism of the surreal." – Locus.

Forthcoming in 2014

The Leena Krohn Omnibus. An unmissable and unstoppable thousand-page celebration of iconic Finnish author Leena Krohn. This epic volume, to be issued in hardcover, trade paperback, and e-book editions, will include the short novels *Pereat Mundus, Tainaron, Dona Quixote & Other Citizens*, and *Gold of Ophir*, among others, in addition to a selection of short fiction, essays, and poetry. The omnibus will also feature appreciations by other writers.

CPSIA information can be obtained at www.ICGtesting.com
Printed in the USA
BVOW08s1458081015

421358BV00002B/176/P